C000157392

The First Sign Of Trouble

A Holly Abbot Mystery

Elinor Battersby

Chapter 1

Perhaps it came from growing up in a household that always had at least one dog, but Holly Abbot had always been an early riser. She was almost always up in time to hear at least the last few bars of the dawn chorus and this morning was no exception. She climbed out of bed and half-heartedly straightened the covers before going for her morning shower. She switched on the water and then, as it warmed up, she stood for a moment examining her reflection in the bathroom mirror. A long winter and a spring spent mostly indoors, sheltering from unseasonable cold, had left her pale and looking tired. Hair of indeterminate colour hung, greasy around her wan face, in desperate need of a wash and condition.

Stepping under the now gloriously hot water she started running through a mental list of everything that she needed to get done that morning. There were the pear tarts to glaze and the paninis to assemble for the local cafe, the brownies and granola squares to slice for the leisure centre and then the biscuits that needed baking and the cupcakes and loaf cakes that had to be baked from scratch. All of this before she even started her deliveries for the day. With a sigh and a regretful look at the untouched bottle of conditioner, she did a quick shampoo, rinsed the suds from her hair and stepped out onto the bath mat.

Damn.

She'd forgotten to grab a towel from the airing cupboard in the hall again. Holly's tiny bathroom didn't allow space for anything more than sink, toilet and shower so she kept the towels in the airing cupboard with the spare bedding. It was a good plan in theory, except that she kept on forgetting to grab one in the mornings on her way to the bathroom, leaving her to do a very cold, damp sprint to grab one on her way back to her bedroom each day. Having completed this she gave herself a cursory rub down and pulled on a pair of joggers, a loose t-shirt and a pair of thick wool socks. One of the benefits of operating her business from home was definitely the relaxed work attire.

Once her feet were safely encased in argyl she was ready to brave the kitchen. It was a beautiful room and it was the whole reason that she'd purchased the flat. The building itself was old and expansive, but had been converted into a number of smaller dwellings. The developers had been somewhat limited in the changes that they could make and still see a profit, so where possible they'd left internal walls where they were and used the existing routes for the gas and plumbing. This had left one of the flats with a tiny bathroom, a minute bedroom, barely any living room to speak of, but a huge kitchen and a tantalisingly low price. For Holly it was absolutely perfect and she leapt on the opportunity. She lived alone, wasn't keen on entertaining and didn't really need space for much besides cooking so for the most part she was very happy with her living arrangements.

Donning her apron she stepped onto the tiled floor, still just barely able to feel the pinch of the cold against the soles of her feet. She set to work methodically, taking the prepared balls of cookie dough from the freezer and transferring them to the oven, preparing the glaze for the tarts while the cookies baked and then moving the hot cookies to a cooling rack and replacing them with the carefully glazed tarts. One task after another with practised efficiency. The oven never stood empty and she seemed to be always beating or whisking or washing up as the counter-tops around her gradually filled with trays and trays of beautiful food.

By 7am she was done and loading up her creations into the dark blue van outside. Starting with the cafe in town and then the leisure centre, she began a winding route from business to business, dropping off her wares to replenish display cases depleted by the breakfast rush. A little over an hour after setting off she had completed her last Cambridge delivery and was on her way back home when she heard the chime of her phone indicating an incoming call. She left it to go to voicemail but a second call followed the first and eventually Holly pulled over to answer.

"Hello darling, are you all done for this morning?" Her mother's voice had a distinct edge to it, her brightness sounding unusually forced.

"Yep, just on my way home now, is something wrong?" Holly asked. It wasn't unusual for her mum to call her for a chat, but this wasn't sounding particularly aimless or carefree.

"We're in crisis over here my love, and I've completely run out of teabags! It's always the way, isn't it? We never run out of tea bags but it's always precisely when you need something that you find that for the first time, there's none left!"

Definitely odd! If she didn't know better, Holly would say that her mother was rambling! The completely unflappable Maggie Abbot, who had raised four children, written umpteen novels and orchestrated the day to day running of her household for three decades was sounding sincerely stressed and calling in reinforcements in the form of her daughter.

"No problem, I'm not far from the village shop, I'll stop in there for some tea and then come straight round," Holly assured her.

The shop was absolutely tiny but somehow still seemed to stock all the essentials. Holly grabbed a pack of fancy ginger biscuits and a large box of Yorkshire Gold teabags and went to pay. Mrs Crevins, the shop's owner, rang it up for her and asked after her parents and her brothers, as she always did. Holly had been purchasing her last minute odds and ends from Mrs Crevins' shop her whole life. On her family's longer walks with the dogs when she'd been little, they'd come out of the woods near here, and she and her brothers would often pool their pocket money to buy a pack of custard creams or maybe a roll of polos to make the walk home feel that much lighter. These businesses, these roads, these walks and this countryside, it was all a part of who she was. She thought, as she often did, of her brothers building their lives all over the country and she couldn't understand how anyone could want to leave.

Her parents' home was a large, rambling affair packed with books, pictures, trinkets and other ephemera collected over the course of a life well lived. Holly knocked on the door, feeling strange as she did, waiting to be allowed entrance to a house that still felt like her home. Her mother answered the door with an anxious expression and preceded Holly through to the kitchen, calling out thanks for the tea bags as she went. Holly followed her into the square room, ringed with scrubbed wooden work surfaces. It was probably about the same dimensions as Holly's own kitchen and yet it felt half the size, filled as it was with bric-a-brac. One counter was stacked with recipe books from various different fad diets. '100 Chicken Recipes' leant against a copy of 'The Modern Vegan' in comfortable companionship. The walls were a hodgepodge of children's drawings spanning 30 years or more. Pots that didn't fit into cupboards had taken up permanent residence on the side next to the hob and there was an impressive collection of jams lined up along one wall out of the direct sun. As her mother busied herself making tea Holly went in search of her father. She found him sitting in the sundrenched conservatory-turned-dining room. He had a newspaper open on the table in front of him but he didn't look as though he was actually reading it. Richard Abbot was a quiet but kind man. He was intensely proud of each of his children, and they in turn, adored him. He'd spent his career teaching secondary school science and so far his retirement had been spent indulging his heretofore neglected creative side. It seemed that every other week he started a new project of some kind and his study was quickly filling up with hand whittled spoons and half finished oil paintings.

"Hello Dad," Holly pulled up a chair and sat down next to her father. He turned and gave her a sad smile.

"Hello Holly love, did your mother call you?" he asked in his gentle voice.

"She did. Apparently you're in crisis over here," Holly told him with a smile, half expecting him to contradict her mother's dramatic words.

"I suppose you could say that," he told her with a sigh.

Holly's brow furrowed with concern. Her father was clearly troubled and wasn't exactly rushing to elaborate as to why. Before she could press him further, her mother swept into the room carrying a tray laden with mugs of tea and a plate of the ginger biscuits that Holly had bought. Holly's family had stopped expecting home-baked goods years ago. Every couple of months Holly would go through the process of developing a new recipe and her parents would be inundated with various versions of the same dish, but apart from these experimental recipes and works-in-progress Holly limited her baking to work or special occasions.

"So, has he told you?" Maggie demanded, setting a mug of tea before each of them. Oblivious to Holly's blank look she continued on in a rush, "Your poor father, I can't believe it! So awful! And that poor man! I can't imagine what could have happened, it's not like he just dropped down dead for no reason, is it?!"

Holly's confusion must have been evident because Maggie turned to her husband with an expression of exasperation and sympathy.

Richard sighed again,

"No Maggie, I hadn't quite got around to saying," he confessed with some chagrin. He turned to Holly and explained quite simply, "I found a body in the woods when I was out walking Rufus this morning."

All eyes turned to the aging border collie reclining in a dog bed in the corner, as though he might be able to shed some more light on the situation. With no response from Rufus, Holly turned her attention back to her father and he in turn turned his attention back to his tea. Holly looked to her mother to fill in the blanks.

"He was walking Rufus early this morning. The daft old thing seems to be waking up earlier and earlier and your dad tends to take him out for a bit of a ramble at about six. Anyway, it seems that this morning they stumbled across some poor fellow who'd been killed! Your dad says that he looked as though he'd been knocked on the head with a rock. It's awful to think of, isn't it? Your dad called the police. They came right out and they kept him there an hour giving his statement! At least it's all done with now though. Poor man, I wonder who he was," Maggie finished with a sad shake of the head.

"It was Terence Wood."

They both turned back to Richard Abbot in surprise.

"You didn't tell me that!" Maggie cried in tones of outrage.

"Did you tell the police?" Holly asked him.

Richard Abbot flushed a deep red and hung his head.

"Richard! You knew who it was and you didn't tell the police?!" Maggie's pitch had now risen to extraordinary levels.

"Why Dad? Why didn't you tell the police that you knew him?" Holly asked, making a valiant effort to keep her own voice calm.

"You knew him too love, he was a couple of years above you at school, Rob's year. He was the boy there was all that trouble with," Richard explained.

A sharp gasp drew Holly's attention back to her mother. Maggie was the sunniest, happiest person Holly knew, but she was also fiercely protective of her family and consequently Terence Wood had been a sore issue for her for years. Holly had known only that Terry Wood was a 'trouble maker', a term that she had later found out referred to drug dealing, truancy and problems with authority. In his role as a teacher, Richard Abbot had come down hard on Terry and had paid the price for it. Terry had set fire to Richard's car in the school car park. Everyone knew that he was responsible and it was generally assumed to be a threat, but as there was no proof, nothing had been done about it. Maggie had been absolutely outraged and the name of Terry Wood had become a curse in their house.

Holly saw the instinctive anger swell at the mention of his name, but just as quickly it faded and Maggie looked anguished, her hands going to her mouth.

"Oh my God! He's Rob's age! He's a baby!" she cried.

Holly did a quick mental review- Rob was... twenty eight. That was young.

"Could it have been an accident?" she asked her father anxiously.

"I don't think so. Like I told your mother, he had a clear head injury and there was a big rock lying right next to him, blood all over it. It didn't exactly look like he just tripped and fell," Richard told her sadly.

"So that's why you didn't tell the police you knew him." Holly gave a low whistle. "They're going to find out though. They'll know you lied."

"I know. It was so stupid, but I just panicked! I knew that it didn't look good, me being the one to find him, so I just... didn't say anything. I was an idiot, I don't know what I was thinking!" He was looking at them imploringly, fear in his eyes.

"They can't possibly think that you were involved though!" Maggie declared, clearly panicking.

"I suspect that that's exactly what they're going to think," Holly told her, pulling out her phone. She dialled in a number and held up a hand, telling her mother to be quiet for a moment.

"Holly?"

"Hi Dan, sorry to bother you but I think that we might need your advice. Dad's in trouble."

As she filled her eldest brother in on the situation, her father buried his head in his hands. The police were almost certainly going to be suspicious. When they found out that he'd known the victim, had a public feud with him and hadn't told them about any of it, the police were going to move him to the top of the suspect list.

Dan was typically pragmatic about it all.

"Tell him to go straight to the police now. He needs to go in voluntarily and tell them everything he knows. He didn't have anything to do with this but when they figure out the connection between him and Terry, they're going to waste time investigating it."

Holly supposed that really she'd known it was the only course of action open to them, but somehow hearing it from Dan, an actual police officer, made it feel more clear cut and straightforward.

She relayed Dan's words to her father and he pushed himself determinedly to his feet, relieved to have a plan of action, even if it wouldn't be an easy one. He pulled a couple of dog treats from his pocket and fed them to the half slumbering collie before pulling on his coat, kissing his wife and daughter and setting off.

Holly spent the next hour attempting to reassure her mother while feeling totally terrified herself. By the time she was back outside and behind the wheel of her van, she was feeling totally drained and her mind was still running a mile a minute.

Instinctively Holly pulled her phone from her pocket and dialled Kat's number. No matter what the crisis, her best friend was always her go-to. Kat picked up on the third ring and after a brief account of Holly's morning, agreed to meet for lunch.

Arriving at the cafe in the centre of town, Holly saw that her friend had beaten her there and managed to snag a table. Wherever she went, Kat tended to draw attention while still managing not to look out of place. Holly had always felt like the opposite, invisible wherever she went, while still managing to look as though she'd stumbled into the wrong venue in the wrong clothes. On the subject of clothes, Holly could already see Kat's critical and disappointed gaze as the bell above the cafe door chimed over her head. She'd swapped her joggers for jeans before setting off on her deliveries that morning but she still looked like she'd assembled her outfit at a jumble sale. Even when she put in the effort, she still never managed to achieve that effortlessly put-together style that her friend seemed to attain so easily, so over time she'd just stopped putting in the effort.

She held up a hand to forestall Kat's inevitable criticism and sat down opposite her, shedding her coat and bag as she did so.

"Ok, ok, fine. I won't say it, but tell me everything! I want details!" Kat demanded.

They got two coffees and ordered a couple of the paninis that Holly had dropped off earlier. While they waited for the food to arrive, Holly filled Kat in on the morning's events, appreciating the perfectly timed gasps and shudders. Kat was nothing if not a wonderful audience. When she got to the part about calling Dan however, Kat interjected.

"You spoke to Dan? Did he say anything?" she asked.

"Well yeah, he said that Dad had to go to the police and tell them everything right away," Holly told her.

"No, not that. Did he say anything about anything else?" Kat questioned.

"No, but when does Dan ever say anything he doesn't need to? He's not exactly chatty, you know him."

The trouble was, Kat did know Dan but she knew a very different Dan than the one Holly was acquainted with. Although neither of them admitted it, Dan was the reason that the two of them were friends. At the tender age of eleven, Kat had caught sight of Dan picking Holly up from school and (as she described it) had practically swooned. She'd invited herself round to Holly's house the next day and despite the fact that Dan was nowhere to be seen, she'd basically never left.

A couple of years later, Dan had moved to London to join the police and he and Kat had barely seen each other again. That was, until Holly's parent's Christmas party last year. At twenty six and thirty three the age gap suddenly didn't seem like such a gulf and without warning something had changed. Holly was still nervous of this development and, perhaps sensing that, Kat wasn't being particularly forthcoming with the details. Holly was living in a state of near constant dread that one day soon her best friend was going to tell her that she was leaving her: her own traitorous brother, whisking away her only friend to a new life in London.

For a moment Holly held her breath... Was it now?.. Was she going to tell her?.. But Kat merely shook out her long blonde hair and said, "Oh well, no matter. So has your Dad gone to the police?"

"Yeah, he went to the station just before I called you. I'm worried though. I know that Dan said it's the right thing to do but I wonder if we shouldn't have got him a lawyer or something. Dan might be putting a bit too much faith in the local police to figure all this out. What if they think that Dad actually had something to do with this? I have to admit, so far it does look suspicious."

Kat considered this for a moment. Dan did tend to have a pretty overwhelming faith and solidarity with the police force.

"Well let's think about this," she said, "Who else would want to bump off Terry Wood?"

It was a good question. He hadn't been an easy person to get along with and the chances were that Richard Abbot wasn't the only person he'd had some kind of conflict with in his twenty-eight years.

Their paninis arrived, toasted to perfection and, for what felt like the first time that day, Holly smiled. She'd opted for pear, brie and caramelised walnut. She'd added a bit of fresh rocket to them and it was utterly delicious. Kat was a bit more traditional in her food choices and was happily tucking into a tomato and mozzarella.

Waiting for her cheese to cool slightly, Holly admitted, "I don't really remember much about him from school and I might have seen him around since but just in passing, not to talk to or anything."

"I remember him from school," said Kat with

conviction. "He was awful. Some people are just horrible and he was like that. He only had friends because he got drugs for the big parties. No idea where he was getting them but he was selling them to loads of people. He dated Kim Dosset for a while in his last year. They got back together again a while back and they live together now."

"Kim Dosset?"

The name rang a vague bell but Holly couldn't place it.

"She was the year above us. She does my nails," Kat told her.

"Do you go to her house?" Holly asked. An idea had occurred to her. Possibly a crazy idea, but really only time would tell.

"Yeah, I've been to hers to have them done before, why?" Kat asked with trepidation.

"So you know where she lives. Good. Take me there!" Holly demanded.

"What?! Why?!"

"I'm not going to do or say anything awful to her; I just want to know more about Terry. At the moment the only person I know who might have hated him was my dad. I just want to get a bit more of an idea of other people who might have a problem with him. I think it would make my mum and dad feel better. Take the pressure off, you know? I expect dad will be home soon and I'd like to be able to tell him something reassuring."

It took some persuading but eventually Kat agreed to take her to visit Kim. Holly didn't have any very clear idea of what she was hoping to find out, she just couldn't stand her father being the only potential suspect that she knew of.

Kim and Terry lived in a small ex-council flat in the rundown little estate that had been grafted onto the east edge of town back in the 1960's. As the size of the town had increased over time it had grown west, away from this estate rather than encompassing it, leaving it like a sore on the outer skin.

There was no lift, so they trekked up the three flights of stairs to an open walkway with flats leading off of it on one side, and the other side having a less than appealing view of another identical block of flats. Over the top of this second block Holly caught a glimpse of trees and she realised with a jolt that she was looking at the far side of the woods where Terry had been found. She'd only approached these woods from the north before, with her family, and she hadn't realised they extended so far. Suddenly her little town felt much smaller.

It was only as they stood waiting outside Kim's front door that a terrible possibility dawned on Holly. What if no one had told Kim about Terry yet?! What if she didn't know that he was dead?!

Faced with the prospect of having to make an impromptu death notification, Holly nearly ran, but before she'd taken a step the door swung open and a vaguely familiar woman stood before her with red, swollen eyes and a tear stained face. Holly froze.

Thankfully Kat- wonderful Kat- stepped into the breach. She moved forwards, words of consolation already flowing from her lips.

17

"Oh Kim, I heard! I'm so sorry!"

The small woman melted into the offered embrace, shaking with sobs. Kat neatly manoeuvred her back into the flat whilst motioning for Holly to follow. The hallway was so narrow that Holly bumped her head on an empty, wall-mounted bike rack and tripped over half a dozen pairs of shoes as they relocated to a kitchen that was so dusty and unloved it made Holly's soul ache. Kat lowered Kim into one of two folding chairs that, together with a really minute formica table, served to take up all the floor space of the room. Kat gestured with her head towards the kettle and then sat down. Holly edged around them with great difficulty to get to the sink and filled the kettle to the brim. Grief definitely called for tea. She discretely started looking for mugs and tea bags while behind her Kat muttered soothing platitudes. Finally, Holly found some cheap crockery and a box of PG Tips. She placed a mug of black tea in front of each of her companions, an exploration of the fridge having yielded nothing more than a stack of budget ready-meals. Holly couldn't stand PG Tips and so she'd decided to go without tea but she was quickly regretting her decision. There was no third chair and barely a foot of space between the table and the kitchen counters so she was left standing awkwardly, right next to Kat's chair, her knees pressed against her friend's leg and her arms hanging uselessly at her sides.

Kat gave her a swift look of exasperation before turning her attention back to Kim.

"How are you doing?" she asked her.

"Not too bad now, at least the police have finally gone. They had some *Support Officer* here this morning to keep an eye on me. They said it was 'to look after me at this difficult time' but I could tell she was just here to snoop. Eventually I told her I didn't want her here, but she still said she's going to come back later to check on me. Nosy cow." Kim told them in a voice tinged with bitterness and exhaustion.

Unused to any open hostility towards the police, Holly couldn't help but wonder if Kim's stance indicated that she had something to hide.

"Do you have any idea who might have done it?" she blurted out suddenly, earning herself a surreptitious kick from Kat. Not for the first time in her life, she was forced to admit to herself that social skills just weren't her strong suit. The look that Kim gave her was condescending bordering on hostile.

"Except your dad you mean?"

Oh. So Kim knew who she was.

"No, no idea. Terry wasn't perfect, but he was doing his best, ya know?" Kim told them.

Kat, with much more tact, asked gently, "I remember him from school Kim, was he still dealing at all now?"

Kim gave a sigh that rang false to Holly.

"I don't know. That's what the police were asking about too but I really haven't any idea. He was always trying to find honest work. He was a handy man and he was always picking up odd jobs, but people made it really hard for him. A lot of people took against Terry for no reason and some people were really awful."

Well this was certainly interesting.

"Who was difficult? Do you know if there was anyone in particular?"

Kim appeared to be thinking for a moment. "Jack, up at the leisure centre. Terry went there looking for work. They took him on to do a bit of cleaning, but after only a couple of weeks Jack turfed him out and told him he wasn't to come anywhere near the place again. Terry said Jack wouldn't even tell him why."

Or possibly, Terry knew exactly why he'd been fired and he just didn't want to tell Kim.

"Was there anyone else? Any other people Terry had problems with?" Holly asked eagerly, but Kim had run out of specifics. She was just sure that people had been against Terry and life wasn't being fair to them. Looking around the dank little flat, Holly couldn't help but wonder if maybe she was right.

"Where else did he work then? If he wasn't dealing, then where was he working? He must have been getting money from somewhere I imagine." Holly knew she'd been too blunt again. She must learn how to converse like a normal human being one of these days. Kim was definitely annoyed and Holly suspected it wouldn't be long before they were shown the door, like that poor Support Officer this morning.

"Look, I told you! I don't know anything about any drugs! Terry worked a bunch of places! He did some bits and pieces around the house for some folk in town: Mrs Peters, Mrs Weiss... maybe others. He worked off and on at the stables for a while last year, and helped out at the garage a few months ago and the youth centre before that. Mostly he just did cleaning, but I know he hoped Pierce at the garage might train him up to be a proper mechanic. The sod never even offered! I told you, people were against Terry!"

Kat tried to smooth things over but there was no hope. Holly had very definitely worn out their welcome and the time had come for them to leave. There was an awkward shuffle as the two seated women attempted to stand but found that they had no space to do so until Holly had retreated into the hall. Then they all made their way back to the front door, a single file of uncomfortable silence.

Once they were back outside Kat made one last attempt at mending some scorched bridges.

"I'm really sorry for your loss Kim. Let me know if there's anything I can do."

Kim nodded her acceptance of the gesture and turned to Holly who hastened to add her own offer of condolence to the mix, but Kim cut her off.

"I liked your dad. He was a really nice teacher. I hope he didn't kill Terry."

With that she turned and closed the door with a snap leaving Holly and Kat standing, lost in the hallway.

Well Kim, thought Holly, that's one thing we have in common.

Holly and Kat didn't say anything more until they were back sitting in the van when Kat turned to her friend and asked, "So did you find out what you wanted to know?"

Holly buried her face in her hands. What had she been

21

expecting? That they would walk in there and Kim would say, 'Oh yes, of course I know who killed him, it was so-and-so who is in no way connected with your family.'?! They had intruded on that woman's grief and asked her if her boyfriend was a drug dealer. Holly just felt sick. She had no right getting involved in any of this, she was a baker! Her dad was probably home from the police station by now, and free and clear of all suspicion. Retired science teachers didn't murder their ex-pupils in the woods!

Chapter 2

Holly dropped Kat off back at her office and then went home. She unpacked all of her empty trays from the back of the van and washed and stacked them on the side to dry. It was only half two but Holly felt like she'd been awake for a week. She lay down on her bed, feeling her aching muscles relax as she let her weight sink down into the mattress. Pulling out her phone, she decided to call her parents and see how her dad had fared at the police station. Maybe she should bake something to take round for them. As tired as she was, her dad would surely be feeling worse after the morning he'd had and it wouldn't take Holly long to put together a cake.

The phone had barely rung before her mother picked up.

"Holly have you heard anything?" Maggie's voice was utterly panicked.

"Mum? Heard about what?" Holly asked.

"Your father!"

"Isn't he home yet?" Holly asked, sitting bolt upright.

"No! It's been hours! I called the police station a little while ago and they wouldn't tell me anything! I asked when he'd be home and they wouldn't say! They can't really think that he's

23

a suspect in all this can they?!"
She sounded so desperate and scared; Holly was in
uncharted territory, feeling utterly useless.
"Oh Mum, I'm sure it'll be fine! I bet they're just really busy
investigating so he probably had to wait before anyone spoke
to him. I expect he's only been in with an actual police
officer for five minutes, and they probably want every little
detail and are writing it all down. He's probably bored out of
his mind but he'll be home soon." Holly hoped that she
sounded convincing because she didn't for one minute
believe her own words. This wasn't exactly a big town and
they didn't have an awful lot of murders. Holly suspected
that her father had been whisked into an interview room the
moment he arrived and the fact that he was still there was a
very bad sign.
After saying goodbye to her mother, Holly headed straight to
the kitchen. She grabbed butter, sugar, eggs, vanilla and
began, almost on autopilot, to make a cake. The scales
remained undisturbed on the counter, she didn't need them
for a basic sponge, she could do it all by eye and feel. As she
creamed the butter and sugar she mulled over everything that
she knew. It wasn't much but it was something. She knew
that Terry had had problems with Jack, the manager at the
leisure centre and possibly other people too. She knew a few
places that he'd worked in the last couple of years doing odd
jobs and cleaning. She also knew that Terry had sold drugs
in school and could have been still selling them now. All of
this information she had obtained while the police were
wasting time questioning her father. Who knew how much

more time they were going to waste? By the time she slid the hot cake out of the oven, she had a plan. Or at least... she had the first few steps of a plan. After that it all became a bit hazy and indistinct.

She left the cake gently steaming on a cooling rack and, grabbing her bag, she headed out the door.

The leisure centre was a huge building, comprising a gym, a swimming pool, badminton courts and a small cafe where parents could enjoy a coffee and some light food while watching their children's swimming lessons through the huge floor to ceiling windows through to the pool. The whole building smelt like chlorine and as far as Holly was concerned that was its saving grace. She never felt comfortable here. Everyone was always decked out in their sports gear and looking flushed but fit. Just stepping through the doors made her feel lumpy and out of shape. She edged uncertainly into the reception area. She dropped off huge trays of food for the cafe a few days each week but on those occasions she darted straight through to the serving counter and handed the trays off to a member of staff. She used post-its on each tray to minimise the need for human contact and she made her escape as quickly as possible, as though fearing that some gym bunny with a high ponytail might try to force her into a pair of leggings if she hung around for too long.

Today Holly had no trays with her and it wasn't even her usual delivery time, so she wasn't completely sure how she was going to get in. To her relief, Holly saw that the receptionist was on a call and so she took her chance. Taking a deep breath and trying to look natural, she pretended to mouth something, pointed at the cafe and swept past with what she hoped was an air of confidence. Once in the cafe she allowed herself to relax a little. This was an oasis in an otherwise hostile land. People sat around drinking coffees and eating cakes or munching on granola squares. She took a deep breath and allowed herself a few seconds to get her bearings. She needed to talk to Jack but she wasn't sure where he would be at this time of day. Did his role as manager mean that he had an office somewhere? Or would he be prowling the gym looking for people who weren't sweating enough? She approached the counter and smiled nervously at the girl working there. It was the same girl who'd accepted the Tuesday morning deliveries for about the last year and Holly was uncomfortably aware that she had no idea what the girl's name was. She decided to just leap right in and hope for the best.

"Hi, is Jack around?" Holly asked.

"Oh hi Holly!"

Bugger.

"He should be around somewhere, you're welcome to head through to the gym and look for him."

Her panic must have been evident because the young server chuckled and relented.

"Tell you what, I'll page him and have him meet you here."

"Thank you, I really appreciate it," Holly told her sincerely, before loitering awkwardly while the girl got in touch with Jack.

"He should be here in about five or ten minutes; he said to get you a drink and something to eat on the house," the girl told her once she'd hung up the phone.

Holly sighed with relief and ordered a latte and one of her own strawberry lemon muffins. She chose a small table on the opposite side of the cafe from the pool viewing seats, and proceeded to pick incredibly slowly at the delicious baked confection. It wasn't just that she didn't feel particularly hungry, she also wanted to make sure that she and Jack stayed here in the cafe rather than moving into any of the other more formidable rooms. This crumbly snack was her plan to keep them anchored to the table and a safe distance from any treadmills or cross-trainers. While she waited she allowed herself to take some time to really appreciate the muffin. It was dense but perfectly moist. The sweetness of the strawberry was balanced by the subtle tang of the lemon. The crumble topping was buttery and rich. It was delicious.

Holly was still smiling when Jack bounded in to the cafe. He was like a Labrador, all energy and enthusiasm. He greeted her with a beaming smile and a vigorous handshake before sitting down opposite her. He raised a hand in signal to the girl working the cafe and a moment later he had a dark green smoothie in front of him. Holly looked at it in horror but Jack just laughed.

"Spinach, kale, apple, flax, celery and pineapple. It's incredible!" he assured her.

He certainly seemed to enjoy it but Holly would have

been hard pressed to imagine a worse drink.

"Thank you for meeting me, I hope it's not too busy a time," she told him.

Jack smiled warmly again.

"It's no bother! I don't think we've exchanged more than a few words since you came on board as a supplier for the cafe! I assume that's what you want to talk about?" he asked.

"Oh! Oh yes, yes of course," Holly stammered, "I wanted to check in and see if everything is alright... with the food."

Jack looked around happily at all of the contented faces.

"I'd say it's all going brilliantly! As you know, we use a few different suppliers for different products, but I'd say your cakes are the definite favourite! At least, with the mum crowd they are. The kids swim classes completely clear out your stock! I wonder if you could put together some healthier options though. In addition to your usual orders of course! Most of the gym goers are straight in and straight out. If they get anything at all they tend to stick to the smoothies but maybe if you could make some healthier treats it would tempt them to stop in for a bite!

Holly was sceptical. She didn't really think of 'healthy' and 'treats' as words that went together. She was never one to back down from a culinary challenge however.

"Absolutely! I'll have a bit of an experiment and drop some samples round to you soon. The cafe really is nice, the whole centre looks... really... nice," she finished feebly.

Holly was well aware of how flimsy this sounded but she wasn't at all sure of how to bring up Terry in a way that would seem even the slightest bit natural. Luckily the leisure centre was a passion of Jack's and he detected nothing amiss in her measly compliment.

"It's fantastic isn't it?!" he enthused, "All our equipment is top of the line and our workout classes are brilliant! It's so important to really take care of ourselves and people just don't seem to realise it! They shovel junk food all day and lay in front of the TV! There's nothing better than getting people moving and getting them healthy! Most rewarding job there is! You know I could totally comp you a workout class if you wanted to give one a go! They're addictive I swear! You wouldn't believe how much better you'll feel!"

Holly mumbled something between a refusal and an evasion and decided that the time had come to turn the conversation before she had a year-long gym membership she'd never use.

"Did I hear that Terry was working here? Was he teaching a workout class?"

The enthusiasm drained immediately from Jack's face and he transformed from excited puppy to wary guard dog.

"No. No he was just cleaning and now he's not working here at all. I didn't realise that you two were friends."

Jack's whole demeanour had changed and he was looking at Holly as though she'd transformed into a cockroach.

"No! No we're not friends!" she hastened to clarify. "We just went to the same school but we weren't even in the same year or anything. I was just making conversation," she assured him, sensing that her job was suddenly on the line.

"Oh." Jack visibly relaxed slightly but the tone of the conversation had definitely changed and Holly could feel the desire to leave radiating from him in waves. He pushed back his chair and was about to stand when he seemed to have second thoughts.

"Terry isn't a good person to make conversation about. People might get the wrong idea about the sort of person you are."

With that cryptic remark he stood to go. He shook her hand again and she promised to drop off some 'healthy treat' samples to him as soon as possible. Even if she hadn't found out anything useful about Terry Wood, at least some good had come out of the meeting. Increased orders were always good for business.

She collected together her coffee cup and the plate from her muffin and walked back to the counter to return them, mulling over her obviously atrocious interrogation and investigation skills.

"Don't mind Jack."

She looked up with a start at the girl behind the counter.

"Sorry?" Holly asked.

"Jack. I was just saying don't worry about him, he's just a proper, die-hard, fitness fanatic so he can't stand people like Terry. Jack can't understand why anyone would put anything unnatural into their bodies and there was no way he was going to have anything like that going on here."

Trying not to sound too excited Holly leaned slightly closer and whispered,

"Drugs?"

Clearly revelling in her newfound air of mystery, the girl just raised her eyebrows slightly, giving Holly a significant look before taking Holly's plate and cup away to be washed.

Holly absent-mindedly thanked her and set off back to her van. Sitting once more in the driver's seat she wondered- had Kim lied? Kim had claimed ignorance of any drug dealing, saying that Terry was working as a handy-man, but the first person that Holly had spoken to had known that Terry was dealing drugs. If Kim had lied, was it to protect Terry's reputation or to protect herself?

And what about Jack? Was his commitment to the leisure centre enough that he might feel he had to get Terry and his drugs out of the picture? So far this was all turning out to be more complicated than Holly had anticipated.

Back at her flat Holly lay sprawled on her bed trying to think through what to do next. The drugs were an interesting angle but they didn't exactly give her a clear direction to go in. The best bet was probably to keep on talking to the people that had been connected with Terry and see if anything came up that might be relevant. She did a quick rundown of the list in her head. The leisure centre could be crossed off for now but that still left the youth centre, the stables, the garage and the elderly Mrs Peters and Mrs Weiss. Not being entirely sure how to track down the old ladies, Holly thought it best to opt for another business first. She'd known Joe who ran the youth centre for most of her life. He would be easier to talk to, but she couldn't imagine him having anything to do with this. She decided to head over to the garage first and talk to Pierce.

The garage was actually half small garage and half small dealership. Either way it wasn't a huge business but it had a good reputation, and if anyone local needed to MOT, repair or to sell their car this was where they came. Holly knew Pierce in the way that you know people who've lived in your small town all your life but their dealings had all been vehicle related rather than social. Holly had purchased her van through him a few years previously and it was to him that she took it if it was ever in need. Unfortunately, her van was currently in perfect working order and she couldn't really justify the expense of getting it looked at just to have an excuse to be there. Holly decided that the direct approach would have to do.

Pierce was just heading out into the lot from the office as she arrived, so Holly flagged him down with a wave.

"Hello Holly! Looking for another van?"

"No, mine is still running great and I really only need the one," she told him.

"Hmm... I've tried your cakes at the cafe in town. When you expand your business you come to me for your second van. I'll be setting you up with a whole fleet eventually, you mark my words!"

Holly couldn't help but beam at the compliment. It was always a great feeling to have her baking appreciated.

"Thank you Pierce. But I'm actually here about something else today," she admitted nervously.

"Alright then, what can I do for you?" He looked at her

expectantly but she didn't know what to say.

Eventually she settled on, "Did you hear about Terry Wood?"

"I did as a matter of fact. I've been expecting the police all day, but I must say I'm surprised to see you here asking about it."

So he knew about Terry. That didn't necessarily mean anything though, word could just be getting around. Either way, it certainly made Holly's job easier.

"My dad found him. In the woods. He's talking to the police now and I just... I don't really know much about Terry so I'm trying to talk to anyone he worked with," Holly explained.

Pierce sighed.

"Well there's another reason for me to regret ever giving him a chance here."

"So you already had a reason to regret it before?" Holly asked quickly.

"I would say so! Before you go thinking it, I didn't bump him off! But I definitely thought about it once or twice," Pierce admitted ruefully. "He was the most lazy and ungrateful employee I ever had the soft-hearted idiocy to hire. He looked askance at everything he was asked to do! He showed up late almost every day on that bicycle of his and then spent the whole time making snide remarks and jabs about not being appreciated for his worth! When people started mentioning that money and other stuff left in cup holders and glove compartments had gone missing, I'd had enough."

"He was stealing?!" Holly didn't know why she was shocked. This all fit together with what Kim had told her, about Terry hoping for a proper apprenticeship and not being offered one. He clearly felt resentful but Holly was still appalled that he would steal people's money and belongings from his own job. It was something that she just couldn't comprehend.

"I've got no proof it was him, but there's no one else it could have been. I tried to ask him about it but he just said he hadn't taken anything. He said people must be confused and hadn't left money or anything there to begin with. I don't have cameras inside the garage building so there was no way to prove anything. He was still in his probationary period so I just didn't keep him on."

"Did you tell the police about it?"

"No, like I said there was no proof. I didn't want to make an enemy of Terry when there was nothing the police could do."

"No I mean today, now that he's dead did you tell them?"

"Well that's just what I was saying when you arrived love. The police haven't been by yet. I was expecting them to be here asking about him but I haven't seen hide nor hair yet. They must have more to go on than an old boss I suppose."

Seeing Holly's anxious look Pierce hastened to reassure her.

"Terry was bad news Holly! Anyone who did him in was doing the world a favour! Anyone who knew him would tell you that!"

This wasn't as comforting as Pierce clearly thought it should be. It wasn't as though people didn't still go to prison for killing lazy drug dealers. She was looking for proof that her dad hadn't killed Terry, not that it was justified if he had!

"Nope, no one thought well of Terry except Joe. I can't understand it, I always thought he was a sensible bloke," Pierce told her, shaking his head in disbelief.

"Joe Dawkins?" Holly asked, puzzled.

"Yep, he was the one who recommended Terry for the job here. I did wonder if he was just trying to get rid of him. I could understand him not wanting Terry hanging around the youth centre. He is a bit of a softie though, so maybe he just wanted Terry to be given another chance."

Either way, Terry had wasted it.

Holly thanked Pierce for his time and left. She hadn't really found much out again, though Terry was definitely being painted a blacker and blacker character. At least she had another direction to move in. Joe Dawkins was the only person who might have had an insight into another, lighter, side of Terry.

She checked her watch, it was getting late. She would stop at home to finish off the cake and then head to her parents' house.

Walking into her flat Holly had to switch on the lights, dusk was falling fast. A shower would have been wonderful, something to wash away the clinging melancholy of the day, but she didn't want to take the time. She settled for changing into a fresh t-shirt and then headed through to the kitchen.

The cake she had backed earlier was still on the cooling rack, a grid pattern pressed into the surface of the perfect, springy sponge. She'd used a double measure of vanilla and the comfortingly sweet scent still lingered in the room. She decided to make a chocolate buttercream for it and grabbed the necessary ingredients. Swapping melted dark chocolate for cocoa powder in the interest of speed, she had the buttercream made and spread generously over the cake in under five minutes. She transferred the whole thing to a tin, grabbed her keys and her phone and headed back out the door. This whole day had been exhausting and it wasn't even over.

Chapter 3

When she pulled up outside her parents' house she could see her mother's anxious face pressed against the window. She was out the front door and hurrying across the driveway before Holly had even got out of the van.

"Have you heard anything? I keep calling them but they're not telling me anything!" Maggie wailed.

Holly scrambled from the van, feet slipping on the gravel driveway, panic robbing her of any grace.

"Mum, are you saying Dad isn't back yet?" Holly asked urgently.

"No! The police still have him!" Maggie confirmed, her voice rising to a truly extraordinary pitch.

Holly ushered her mother back into the house, handing her the cake tin and pulling out her phone.

Maggie took the tin through to the kitchen and put it on the side amidst all the other bits and bobs that had turned up there during the course of the day. Holly followed her, dialling Dan's number.

"Hi Holly, how did Dad get on?" he asked her calmly.

"We don't know Dan! They haven't let him go!" she cried.

There was a pause as Dan processed this, then-

"What time did he go to the station to talk to them?" he asked.

"As soon as I spoke to you this morning! He went straight in and they haven't let him out! Mum's been calling them all day and they won't tell her anything!"

"But that was hours ago! Oh Christ! Give me five minutes."

He hung up. Holly looked at her mum, waiting anxiously, her face strained and her eyes tired.

"He's going to sort it. Don't worry mum, he's Dan."

Maggie crumpled in on herself, her body racked with sobs as her control finally snapped. Stepping forward Holly wrapped her arms around her and held her while she cried. It was a strange reversal of roles; her mother was such a force of nature and so rarely seemed to need anyone. Holly could only be grateful that she was here for her when she suddenly did.

After a few minutes Maggie stepped back and gave her daughter a warm smile.

"Thank you darling."

Holly felt tears just starting to prick her own eyes when her phone rang. She fumbled to answer as quickly as she could.

"Hello? Dan?"

"It's alright Holly, I called your local station and talked to the detective in charge of the investigation. It seems that the regular Chief Inspector left recently and this guy is just a temporary replacement who wasn't supposed to be on duty today. Apparently it took some time for him to arrive and then he had to get caught up before talking to Dad." Dan explained.

Holly was just working herself up into a righteous fury when Dan cut her off.

"I know Holly, they should never have treated Dad like that. It seems to me that the case is already being mismanaged and they're acting like a bunch of idiots."

Holly had never heard her brother talk disparagingly about fellow officers before and she wasn't really sure what to say. Dan's unwavering faith in the police as a source of all that is just and good had been a constant in Holly's life. Every Halloween had seen Dan dressed in some variation on a police uniform. He had been a detective, a uniformed officer, a sheriff and one year in a slight deviation from theme, Sherlock Holmes. No one had been surprised when he announced his intention of joining the police force straight out of university, but they had been sad to see him go.

Somehow, hearing Dan criticise police actions had the effect of calming Holly down.

"Well at least they're going to let him go now. They are going to let him go aren't they?" she asked.

"He should be out of there in the next few minutes and on his way home. Give me a call if there's anything else you need and give Mum a kiss for me. Tell her I'll call her tomorrow."

As Holly filled her mother in on what Dan had said they both moved slowly around the kitchen, Holly tidying up and her mother preparing some soup. Holly sorted through discarded papers and envelopes while Maggie chopped vegetables. Holly put away tupperware and cleared the draining board while her mother boiled stock. With the soothing efficiency of practised teamwork they got the house back in order and a pot of glorious smelling soup on the table with a loaf of crusty white bread and salted butter. By the time Holy heard her father's jeep outside she was feeling positive and in control again. This feeling lasted right up until she answered the door.

"Sorry love, I forgot my key."

He looked exhausted. Standing there in the doorway, evening having arrived in his absence, Holly had never seen her father look so small. The usually soft lines of his face seemed to have been etched in. His eyes seemed heavy with the weight of a long, hard day. Holly felt another wave of anger surge up within her. How could the police put her father through this?! Her quiet, gentle father, the man doing oil paintings of cats and coaxing runner bean plants out of the ground. But deeper than that there was an anger at the person who was the root of all of this. Someone had beaten Terry Wood to death with a rock and left his body to be found in the woods. That person had to pay.

Holly and her mother ushered Richard quickly inside and into the warm conservatory. Even through his evident exhaustion the sight of the fresh soup standing steaming on the table brought a smile to his face. Maggie got him settled in his usual chair and ladled a generous portion of beautiful orange soup into his waiting bowl before she and Holly sat down around him. They waited with baited breath as he dipped a piece of bread in the delicious concoction and placed it almost reverently into his mouth. The grey tinge to his skin receded and he looked to Holly like himself again as he smiled and enthusiastically tucked into his meal.

With the first bite Holly realised how hungry she was. She'd had a panini with Kat and a muffin with Jack but that was, in her opinion, nowhere near enough food for a full day! Her mother's vegetable soup was one of her favourite meals. It was just spicy enough and just rich enough whilst still being creamy and mellow. Despite being a relatively healthy vegan dish Holly felt that it nestled somewhere between comfort food and haute cuisine. They chatted as they ate, about inconsequential things and general news. Maggie said how nice it was to hear from Dan but that was as close as they got to touching on the darkness of the day. Holly felt herself relax in a way that was only possible for her in this house, with these people. This was probably why her little flat remained basically undecorated and barely furnished, this was still her home.

Soup was followed by cake and cups of tea and before she knew it, night had fallen. Looking out the window at the pitch black Holly eyed her mother hopefully. Maggie smiled indulgently in response.

"Yes dear, you can sleep here."

A wave of relief carried her up the stairs and into her old room. It still looked the same except for the now almost empty wardrobe and chest of drawers. Holly dug out a night dress from the heavily depleted store of clothing and went into the bathroom to change and get ready for bed. She could hear her parents moving around downstairs and she thought that there had never been a more comforting sound. She fell asleep almost as soon as her head hit the pillow and her dreams were only briefly troubled by prison cells and battered skulls.

Holly woke to bright sunlight streaming through yellow curtains. During their schooldays Kat had always insisted that waking up in Holly's room was an assault to the senses. Yellow walls and yellow curtains was, admittedly, a decidedly bold look for a bedroom but Holly had always loved it. And the sounds of the dogs barking, her brothers shouting and many feet thundering up and down the stairs had always made Holly feel like she belonged. These days the mornings were a much quieter time but the feeling of belonging hadn't diminished. Holly rose and washed up in the bathroom before pulling on a mixture of her clothes from the day before and the odd garment of clean clothing sourced from what she'd left behind when she moved out. She walked downstairs in slightly grubby jeans and a bright green 'Explore The Wilderness' t-shirt that had been huge on her when she'd bought it on a day out to an RSPB reserve as a pre-teen, but now fit a little more snugly than she'd have liked.

Thursdays were Holly's day off so she hadn't bothered to set an alarm the night before. Checking the time on her phone she saw that it was almost 8am, an impressive lie-in by her usual standards. As she walked past the study door she could hear her father clattering about inside, no doubt commencing his next journey of creative self-exploration. Through the kitchen window she could see her mother in the garden, sitting in one of their wrought iron chairs, watching Rufus the dog snuffle about investigating the flower bushes.

Holly put a couple of pieces of bread in the toaster and then put the kettle on for tea. She found an open jar of apricot jam in the fridge and she soon had a tray ready. She took the two mugs of tea and plate full of toast outside and set them on the table. Sitting down opposite her mother she asked,

"What are you up to Mum?"

"Just a spot of gardening dear. Ooh is that tea for me? Lovely!"

They both leant back in their chairs for a moment, sipping their tea.

"Wait, did you say gardening?" Holly asked.

"Yes darling," Maggie cheerfully confirmed.

Holly looked at her mother. Gardening was looking an awful lot like sitting in the garden enjoying the sunshine. Finally her mother huffed slightly and explained.

"Your father keeps being 'busy' all the time with his projects! It makes me feel unbearably lazy! It's fine when I have writing to do but I'm waiting for some pages back from my editor at the moment, so instead I tell him I'm gardening and I come out here. It's just as well the weather's nice."

Holly chuckled and resumed the contented drinking of her tea and munching of toast. Her mother had been a secretary of some kind before giving up work during her first

43

pregnancy, whereupon she had immediately commenced work on her first book. She now had eighteen novels published and Holly was the only one of her children to have ever read a single one of them. Holly had read her mother's first novel when she was fifteen and that had been quite enough for her. Maggie Abbot wrote bodice rippers. They were vastly popular and her children were very proud and totally mortified all at once. It hadn't been easy at school when people had got wind of what her mother did, but it had still been easier than her father being the science teacher. Holly's brothers all seemed to be cheerfully unruffled by any teasing but Holly, already naturally quiet, had ended up very shy.

Holly had always been happiest at home in the kitchen. She'd started cooking and baking with her parents and her brothers when she was about three years old, and it had immediately become her favourite activity. As she'd got older and started to think about the future, baking had seemed like the obvious career choice for her. She'd been building up her client base slowly from the time that she was a teenager, and by the time she'd graduated from sixth form college she was able to support herself with her cooking. For Holly this was a dream come true. She got to spend her time making delicious food, she was close to her parents and she had Kat. Life was pretty much perfect. A lot of Holly's peers had gone off to university but Holly couldn't see the appeal. She was working for herself so she didn't need a degree, and she had no inclination to move away for three years racking up a monstrous amount of debt. Kat had gone to university but she'd stayed local so that she could keep living at home and keep costs down. Holly would probably never earn as much as Kat would at her fancy office job, but at least Holly would never have to complain about lazy co-workers or unreasonable bosses. All in all, sitting out in the garden with her mum on a beautiful morning, Holly was very happy with her life. If only this pesky murder issue could be sorted out.

Chapter 4

After much umming and ahhing, Holly decided that she would still go and talk to Joe at the community centre. Her father had eventually been released but even Dan had admitted that the case wasn't being handled well, and the police didn't seem to know what they were doing. She didn't want to risk her father ending up in prison just because the local police turned out to be incompetent. If they seemed to be focusing on Richard Abbot, Holly wanted to be ready to point them in the right direction. Finishing off the last of her toast, Holly kissed her mother goodbye and headed back into the house. She gathered up her stuff, said goodbye to her dad and headed out.

The youth centre was a large, sprawling building all on one level. It consisted of a large hall, a small hall, an outdated kitchen and a small warren of offices, store rooms and meeting rooms. The halls and meeting rooms were rented out for things like dance classes, charity functions and birthday parties. There were also some regularly scheduled sports clubs and classes that Joe ran each week, and the rest of the time it served as a sort of drop-in for kids in town to come and meet friends or have a kick about. Holly herself had taken ballet classes here as a child, helped out at a number of charity functions and watched her brothers play countless hours of ball games with their friends. Holly parked her van next to the empty bike rack and went in. She followed the sound of children shouting, and found the large hall swarming with ten year olds in gym gear. There were two adults shouting out instructions and blowing whistles but neither of them was Joe, so Holly continued along the corridor past the kitchen and on to Joe's office. She knocked and heard Joe's typical cheery shout from inside,

"Just a mo'! Be right with you!"

The door opened and Joe's smiling face appeared.

"Holly! Of course! The perfect person!"

"I'm sorry?" This wasn't quite the temperate reception Holly was used to.

"I'm in crisis Holly! Thirty people coming for a sit down dinner, and no food! Well no, that's not quite true, the food is all ordered but the bloody caterer has bailed on me! Unless I'm going to serve the donors raw spuds, I'm in trouble!"

Ah! This was a crisis that had some real potential for Holly! She'd done a few dinners in the past and she loved it but it wasn't an opportunity that presented often.

"When's the dinner Joe?" she asked.

"Saturday night. I know that's not much notice but the caterer called first thing this morning and said she's come down with something. She's given me a few suggestions of people I could call but truth be told I'd rather give the job to you if you're available?"

"I'd love to Joe! Do you have a copy of the menu and all

the food that's been ordered?"

"I definitely do..." he turned and looked into his strangely bare office "...somewhere."

On previous occasions when Holly had seen Joe's office, the desk and every other surface in the room had been covered with papers and notebooks. Holly had wondered then how Joe managed to find anything, now she wondered where all the papers had gone! This question was answered when Joe opened his desk drawers. Holly could see that far from organising, Joe appeared to have swept everything into these drawers and out of sight. She could see that the desk had been cleaned though so she decided it was an improvement of sorts. Seeing her gaze, Joe smiled ruefully.

"I'm not much one for cleaning I'm afraid. I thought I'd have a stab at it though. Saturday is a dinner for the centre's investors and they often want to have a look around."

Finally he found the printout of the menu and the receipts for the food.

"The delivery should be arriving here at 9am but I can put it in the fridges and you can come any time to do all the cooking bit and stuff."

Cooking bit and stuff? This really wasn't Joe's strength.

"Sounds lovely! Depending on my deliveries that morning I should be here not long after nine myself," she told him.

"Fantastic! But unless you've developed some psychic powers, Saturday's dinner isn't what brought you round here. What can I do for you?" he asked, smiling.

Holly had almost forgotten her original intention in the

excitement. It flooded back in now and her smile faded.

"Have you heard about Terry, Joe?" she questioned cautiously. Joe didn't say anything, just looked at her nervously so she pressed on. "He's been killed Joe. In the woods near my parents' place."

Joe sighed slightly, "Oh God."

"I'm sorry. You're the only person I've heard liked him, it must be a shock," she offered.

Joe did look shocked. He looked like he didn't really know what to say or what to do with himself.

"I did like him, he wasn't a bad guy. Poor Terry. He had a rough time, I just thought he deserved a chance," he told her.

"Is that why you recommended him to Pierce at the garage? And you got him odd jobs from a couple of other people too, didn't you?" Holly queried.

"Just a couple of people from church who needed a hand. It wasn't a big deal." Joe was looking at her warily now. He was wondering why she was asking all of these questions. She couldn't bear for Joe to think that she suspected him!

"I just wondered if someone should let them know about it. So they know not to expect him round." Holly told him.

Joe's face cleared. "Oh! That's a good point! I'll be sure to tell them, it'll be better coming from me. Thank you Holly" He looked grateful and Holly's insides squirmed.

Holly wasn't sure if the police would be thrilled not to be breaking the news to people themselves, but she decided not to say anything. If the police were going to get in a huff about it then they should be the ones here investigating. She thanked Joe again for the catering job and left, promising to see him Saturday morning.

Holly sat outside in her van wondering how on earth the police did it. She hadn't asked Joe how he knew Terry, when the last time he saw him was or if he knew of any problems Terry was having. Really, she hadn't asked anything. Holly had chickened out and left herself in a dead end. She didn't even know who the elderly people were that Terry had worked for. She contemplated going back in and trying again but really she didn't think that she could face it. She wished that there were fewer people involved that she knew. Holly was sure that her dad hadn't done anything wrong but she couldn't imagine Kim, Jack, Pierce or Joe as cold-blooded killers either.

What was it Joe had said? 'Just a couple of people from church.'

She pulled out her phone,

"Hey, Mum? I need a favour."

She could hear the tap running in the background and the gentle clatter of crockery.

"Of course darling!" her mother cried in a sing-song voice, "Wonderful to be needed! How may I be of assistance?"

"You go to the same church as Joe Dawkins don't you? Do you know a Mrs Peters and a Mrs Weiss?"

"Hmm... I know them just to say hello to in passing but I wouldn't say we're close." Maggie told her.

"Do you think you could get hold of their addresses?"

Holly asked.

Her mother paused.

"I probably could darling, we have addresses on file for our elderly congregation and I could probably track them down... but why are you asking?"

Holly wasn't sure how to explain. She hadn't told her mother that she was looking into Terry's death. For one thing, she was a baker and was a little embarrassed at her own presumption. She didn't want to appear to be claiming to be some kind of super sleuth! She also suspected that her mother might not be thrilled with the idea of her pursuing a killer. On the off chance she actually found them, it might prove not to be the safest thing in the world.

"I was just talking to Joe and he mentioned them. Terry Wood worked for them both and I thought I might drop round some cake or biscuits or something to make them feel better."

"Hmm... well that's a lovely idea. So let's just both pretend that I believe you and I'll see if I can find those addresses. I'll message them to you when I've tracked them down, okay darling?"

"Thanks Mum."

Holly had never been brilliant at lying to her mum and Maggie had already had four boys to teach her to be mistrustful by the time Holly came along. Holly tended to just tell her mum the truth, or at least as close to the truth as she was able. To that end Holly set off home to put together some treats for the Mrs Peters and Weiss.

As she reached her flat Holly's phone rang.

"Holly? What are you up to? I'm on lunch and I have to get out of the bloody office!"

"Hey Kat, I'm just about to do a bit of baking, you can come round to mine if you like."

"Amazing!" her friend enthused, "I'll be there soon!"

Holly rummaged through her food stores looking for something to inspire her. Ah! Lemons! Perfect! Holly had a wonderful recipe that she'd painstakingly developed for lemon shortbread biscuits and they were too crumbly to sell to any of the cafes so she hardly ever got to make them. Bearing in mind that Kat was headed over, she tripled the recipe. These small biscuits were little round bites of lemony, buttery, melt-in-your-mouth heaven and she and Kat had been known to devour an entire batch in about 5 minutes flat. She had the dough whipped up in no time and was already forming the small rounds when Kat arrived in her usual whirlwind of energy. She threw her jacket and bag onto the armchair and flopped down onto the sofa with her legs kicked up over the arm. The whole time she was talking a mile a minute about Lance at the office being a weasel, the weather being gorgeous, Holly's flat being too small and Kat herself being absolutely famished.

Holly frowned affectionately at the sight of her friend sprawled out like some damsel in distress about to expire from hunger.

Fully aware of Kat's capacity for cookies, Holly threw her a banana to tide her over and resumed filling the baking sheet with cookie dough. Whilst the first batch baked she filled another tray and then another.

Chapter 5

"Got any wine?"

"What?! Kat it's lunchtime!"

"If you knew the morning I've had you'd understand! It feels like at least 8 o'clock to me!"

Holly laughed but she knew better than not to take her friend seriously. Crossing over to the fridge she poured her friend a half glass of Chardonnay and poured an inch for herself.

"Ooh! Thank you! What is that?!" Kat demanded.

"What?" Holly asked, puzzled.

"That shirt Holly!"

Holly looked down at herself and saw that she was still wearing the green RSPB shirt that she'd snagged from her bedroom at her parents' house.

"It's nothing," she assured her friend.

"It's fitted! I can see you have a waist! And other things besides!! Please tell me there's a boy," Kat cried enthusiastically.

"There is not a boy. I stayed at my parents' house last night and I don't have all that many clothes there anymore," Holly explained.

Kat visibly deflated. "One day there had better be a boy. Or girl, your choice, just so long as you have someone so that we can double date."

Holly held her breath. Was this it? Was Kat going to tell her that she was moving to London to be with Dan full time?

But Kat just took another sip of wine and wandered into the kitchen.

"So where are my treats? I was promised treats!" Kat called.

Just then the oven timer trilled and Kat beamed. "Perfect!"

They managed to rein themselves in from eating more than the one batch of shortbread, but only just. Once they cooled Holly boxed up the remaining two batches ready for Mrs Peters and Mrs Weiss. Her mother hadn't come through with the addresses yet but Holly was still hopeful. Sat on the sofa, their feet curled up underneath them, Holly filled Kat in on who she had spoken to and what she'd learned so far.

"I can't believe Dan was critical of the police! That's definitely interesting. Did he say much else?"

"He couldn't have been anything BUT critical!" Holly countered. "It is unlike him though."

Kat was looking decidedly thoughtful.

"There isn't exactly an obvious answer yet is there."

"No, in a lot of ways I feel no closer at all. There is something at the edge of my mind though. Something's bothering me but I can't quite figure out what it is."

Kat was looking at Holly's puzzled face, half amused,

half impressed.

"I guess just keep on talking to people. You haven't been to the stables yet?"

"No." Holly responded, "it's on my list but I haven't gotten around to it yet."

"And this has nothing to do with you being terrified of horses?"

"I am not terrified of horses!" She absolutely was. "I am suitably cautious!" No, she was terrified.

"If you want I could come with you. I could call in sick to the office and we could go this afternoon. I haven't taken a single sick day so far at that job, it might be good for them to have a chance to miss me."

Holly was definitely tempted. Now that she'd agreed to cater the meal at the youth centre her Saturday was totally booked and her Friday was going to be twice as busy, to get all of her usual work for Saturday done too. This might be the best opportunity to go out to the stables and, if she was totally honest with herself, it would be nice to have someone with her when she was going to be around horses. That being said, she didn't want to get Kat in trouble.

"Are you sure? I don't want you getting in trouble at work because of me."

Kat gave a nonchalant half shrug. "It'll be fine, let's go."

As Kat called her boss to let her know that she wouldn't be back in until tomorrow, Holly couldn't help but wonder if this new relaxed attitude to her employment was a sign that Kat was going to be leaving her job soon anyway. If Holly were braver she would just ask Kat outright if she was planning to leave, but currently she wasn't ready to hear it. Even this state of tension and uncertainty was better than saying goodbye to her best friend.

The stables were only about twenty minutes outside of town but it was a lovely drive. It was all small, winding roads, so narrow that the trees on either side had stretched out their branches to meet in the middle in a green canopy casting dappled light over the cars beneath. Holly drove them in her van because, besides the wine, Kat hated driving on roads like these. Whilst Holly was enjoying the trees and flowers, Kat was dreading cars coming the other way. Despite Kat's fears they reached the stables unscathed. Holly pulled into the small car park and took her time stowing her keys in her bag, putting on her jacket and finally, reluctantly, getting out of the van.

At the age of seven Holly had decided that she loved horses. She had previously shown absolutely no interest in the equine species, but now she was intent on becoming a show jumper. She drew pictures of horses and wrote about horses and talked about horses and kept up an incessant stream of requests for horse patterned bedding, note books and stickers. She started each morning by asking her parents to buy her a horse and spending the duration of breakfast time trying to think of the perfect name for her future pet.

Holly's parents very sensibly decided that rather than the purchase of a show jumping marvel, horse riding lessons might be the most sensible first step. Holly had never been so excited as the first day they brought her to the stables.

This excitement had lasted right up until she met Cupcake, a beautiful chestnut mare. When the instructor had attempted to lift Holly onto Cupcake's back, Holly had started screaming and crying so loudly that she'd very nearly set off a stampede. Everyone had agreed that horses might not be Holly's thing after all and she decided that actually, cupcakes of the baked variety might be more her speed.

Catching sight of Kat's amused smirk, Holly assumed what she hoped was an air of cool unconcern. She looked around her and was surprised to see how little had changed in a couple of decades. The woman who had owned the stables when Holly was a child had retired almost three years ago and Sandra Dawkins, Joe's younger sister had taken over management of the place. Although Holly didn't know Sandra well, she had met her a couple of times, so at least she knew who she was looking for. There was no obvious reception area so they just edged forwards, vaguely hoping that someone would appear soon and offer assistance.

Holly could see a couple of very young girls riding their horses around the paddock at a brisk trot and tried to tell herself that if they weren't afraid, she certainly had no cause to be. Still, she was very relieved when Sandra exited a stall to their left and came towards them.

"Hi there! Can I help you ladies?" she called.

The resemblance to her brother was immediately apparent. They had the same blue eyes, straight nose and the same wide, open smile.

"We'd like riding lessons," Kat cheerfully informed her.

"No! No we wouldn't!" Holly turned and glared at Kat who smiled back at her with wide, innocent eyes.

Sandra had reached them now and was looking good-naturedly from one to the other of them. Holly rallied and dove right in.

"Sorry, I don't want to be a pest but if you have a minute I'd like to talk to you about Terry Wood."

Sandra looked nervous and confused and something else...

"I'm sorry, why? What's going on?" Sandra asked.

"I heard that he worked here a while ago doing odd jobs," Holly probed.

"Who told you that?"

Sandra was not being particularly forthcoming so far.

"His girlfriend, Kim, mentioned it," Holly explained.

"So what, you're looking for a reference or something?"

Suddenly it dawned on Holly that Sandra was missing some key information here.

"No, Sandra, Terry is dead. He was killed in the woods a couple of days ago. I'm sorry, I thought you knew, I thought that Joe would have told you."

"Joe?" Sandra looked stunned. She'd turned pale and there was a look that Holly couldn't identify. It wasn't getting any easier to break bad news to people.

"Yes, I told Joe this morning. I assumed he'd have called you, I know they were friends."

Sandra looked scornful and surprised, "They weren't friends!"

"Didn't Joe recommend Terry to you?"

Sandra was looking confused again, like Holly was speaking in some kind of code that she hadn't been given the key to.

"What are you talking about?!"

Sandra was sounding less than patient now so Holly decided to get to the point.

"Kim said that Terry worked here doing odd jobs. Is that true?"

"Yes, but not for ages now. He stopped at the beginning of last year, I haven't even really seen him since."

"So you don't know of anyone having problems with Terry? Any trouble?"

"No. I don't know anything about Terry or about what's happened to him."

Perhaps realising that she was being somewhat hostile, Sandra softened slightly. "I'm sorry. It was months ago, after my fall, I don't think I can tell you anything useful."

"Fall?"

Sandra laughed and her brow cleared. Suddenly she was her brother's sister again, light hearted and cheerful.

"I took a tumble off the back of Clearsky." She grimaced at the memory. "She was startled by a dog and reared up. I landed on the road and broke my leg in two places. It was so embarrassing!"

Embarrassing wasn't exactly the word Holly would have chosen. She was staring at Sandra in open mouthed horror but Sandra only chuckled again.

"I know! When you ride horses you're taught to fall without hurting yourself but I was just unlucky with the camber of the road."

Taught to fall?! What kind of activity was this?! Holly was feeling utterly horrified. Thankfully Kat stepped in before Holly could beg Sandra to find a new vocation.

"Holly isn't a horse person, she's too much of a chicken."

"I am not a chicken! I have a healthy respect for my personal safety!"

Sandra and Kat both laughed and Holly flushed slightly. Time to get back on topic.

"So that was why Terry started working here? You needed help after the accident?"

Sandra hesitated for a moment, perhaps reluctant to admit to any weakness.

"Yes. Not right away of course. First I had to have surgery on my leg and then there was some rehab so the stables were closed to the public for a while anyway. It was a couple of months later I hired Terry. It wasn't a lot, just once a week or so Terry would cycle out here and do a bit of work around the place." Sandra looked nervous again. "Cash in hand, you know?"

So perhaps that was it, Terry hadn't been an official employee and Sandra didn't want to get into legal issues for paying him off the books? That could certainly explain why Sandra had been so reluctant to talk to them when they'd first asked about Terry.

Holly didn't want to press the issue and she thought that they'd probably learned all that they could for now. If her mother still didn't have those addresses for her then maybe she'd go home and start getting some of her Friday orders ready now, to give herself as much time to prep for Saturday as possible.

They thanked Sandra for her time and walked back to the car park. Once they were back in the safety of the van Kat let out a long breath and turned to Holly.

"Do you feel like we *only just* got away from that without a full-on argument?"

Holly thought back to Joe's face when she started asking him questions about Terry and sighed.

"People don't like to be accused of doing something wrong. I don't know how Dan does this for a living."

"He hates that part of the job. He knows it's all part of helping people but it makes him feel lousy." Kat told her.

Holly looked up at Kat in surprise. This unexpected insight into her brother's feelings made her feel closer to him, but also further away. Kat shared an understanding with Dan that Holly couldn't even really comprehend. She'd never had a real relationship herself and watching Kat and Dan get closer and closer made her feel isolated from them both. Not sure what to say, Holly decided to just change the subject.

"I should get home, I need to start cooking for tomorrow now that I've agreed to the catering job on Saturday."

Chapter 6

Arriving back at her flat, Holly threw her bag down onto a chair and flopped onto the sofa in a huff. Eventually she would have to talk to Kat about what her plans for the future were but she knew that when she did she would need to be supportive. Dan and Kat were both important to her and she loved them both. She knew that she should be happy for them and she wished that she could be, but at the moment she was still feeling grumpy and resentful about the whole thing. She briefly considered whether she should move to London too, but she knew that she wouldn't; her heart was here and she just didn't feel any desire to leave. Holly could never understand why her brothers had left. Each of them had gone off to university and never returned. They visited of course, but it wasn't the same. Home was home to Holly and she wasn't going anywhere.

This self indulgent melancholy wasn't going to get her anywhere. Holly pulled herself together and got up off the sofa. What she needed was time to think and devise a plan of action. Nothing helped to focus the mind quite like cooking and luckily Holly had an awful lot of food to prepare if she was going to be ready for Saturday. She was excited about the event and it felt terribly dull to make the same old recipes when she knew she was going to be doing something new in a couple of days, but the food for the dinner wouldn't be arriving until Saturday morning and she had all of the orders for her regular customers to take care of before then. Putting aside thoughts of Saturday's dinner, Holly settled herself into the comforting rhythm of her routine tasks. She part baked bread rolls for paninis while slicing tomatoes, cheddar, brie, pears and other delicious ingredients to fill them with. She assembled trays and trays of them and then transferred them all to the huge industrial fridge freezer that stood against one wall. Cupcakes needed to be baked as fresh as possible but pastry could be prepared ready for cinnamon whirls and raspberry croissants and custard rounds. Cookie dough was best prepared and then frozen in evenly sized domes so that the cookies didn't spread too much upon baking. Frozen (or at least chilled) cookie dough produced taller, more decadent cookies than most fresh doughs could achieve.

Holly made dozens and dozens of balls of milk chocolate chip cookie dough, sprinkled with sea salt. She made huge batches of white chocolate and freeze dried raspberry dough and great quantities flavoured with Sicilian orange extract, fresh zest and studded with dark chocolate chips. Gazing into the now fully stocked fridge and freezer Holly was happy with the amount that she'd completed. She'd had to be creative with fitting everything in and had extricated some frozen chicken breasts from the freezer in order to make more room. She now put these into the oven with some tomatoes, peppers, garlic and tarragon to roast and put some rice into a pan to boil. She wasn't feeling particularly hungry, she never did while she was baking, but she knew that once the food was ready she would feel suddenly ravenous. She'd been baking for hours and the evening was now well advanced. She knew that she had about twenty minutes before her dinner would be cooked and maybe a little more for it to cool enough for her to eat, so she decided to measure out cupcake ingredients ready for the morning. She grabbed an assortment of bowls and measured butter and sugar into half of them and flour and baking powder into the other half. She had just finished stretching her reusable covers over each of the bowls when the timer went for her evening meal.

She put her perfectly fluffy rice onto a plate, placed the chicken breasts on top and poured the chunky sauce that the roasted vegetables and chicken juices had formed over the top.

Finally, she poured herself a large glass of white wine and moved to the sofa, snagging a notebook and pen on the way that she usually used to keep track of shopping requirements.

While she was baking Holly's mind had been running though everything that had happened since she found out that her father had found Terry Wood's body. She'd been back over everyone she'd spoken to and everything they'd said. She realised now that she hadn't been asking the right questions. Scared of offending people, she'd barely asked any questions at all really. Holly hadn't asked anyone when they'd last seen Terry. She hadn't asked anyone what they'd been doing on Tuesday night or Wednesday morning.

There were some other questions that needed answering too. What was Terry doing in the woods? Could he have been meeting someone there to do a drug deal? If so, was he buying drugs or selling them? It would be nice if all of this could be chalked up to some drug deal gone bad and not have anything to do with Holly's family or friends, though Holly wasn't sure how to go about finding out where the drugs Terry sold came from. A more basic question was, who benefited from Terry dying? And lastly, Holly had realised what it was that had been bothering her. The woods where Terry had been found were to the east of town. If you walked north through them you came to the long rambling road that Holly's parents' house was on. If you walked west through them you walked through increasingly middle class residential areas towards the town centre. If you walked south through them you came to the estate where Terry and Kim lived. She remembered seeing the tops of trees on the other side of the next block of flats. The distance from Terry's front door to the edge of the woods couldn't be more than a couple of hundred meters. So where was Terry's bike?

Sandra and Pierce had both mentioned Terry cycling to work. The estate where he lived wasn't the sort of place where you left a bike outside, chained up or not. Holly had hit her head on a wall mounted bike rack in the hallway of Kim and Terry's flat, but there had been no bicycle in attendance. Holly had to admit that she couldn't immediately see why it would be relevant, but the fact that she didn't know where it was troubled her. Surely Terry wouldn't have cycled to his wooded rendezvous? At the first opportunity Holly would have to check around the woods on the estate side and see if there was any evidence of a bike. It was always possible that Terry had left his bike there and it had already been stolen though. Holly pulled out her phone and did a quick search on Gumtree and similar sites for any bicycles for sale in town. There were a number of children's bikes and stationary exercise bikes, but nothing else. She set an alert for any new adult bike listings and put the phone away.

So, still on her list of things to do there was:

- Checking for the bike
- Speaking to Mrs Peters
- Speaking to Mrs Weiss
- Speaking to Kim again (at the very least she needed a description of Terry's bike)
- Finding out more about Terry's drug dealing. This was a bit vague but really Holly wasn't sure how to go about it and she was just hoping that something would become obvious.

Holly had prepared almost everything ready for her Friday customers, but she also needed to bear in mind that alongside her investigating she had to deliver all of her orders for tomorrow and then start prepping all of her Saturday orders, to leave Saturday free for the Youth Centre dinner.

Feeling like she finally had a plan and a direction Holly polished off her dinner and headed to bed. She didn't like eating so late and her dreams were troubled again. A nightmare formed around her in which she discovered that everyone she knew had been buying drugs and now they all stood in a circle shouting that she was sending them to jail. Terry himself walked through the group in a smart suit handing out business cards and offering to act as legal representation. As Holly frantically recommended that people engage actual lawyers rather than hiring Terry, her friends and family started to transform one by one into horses that grew taller and taller and towered over her.

It was with relief that Holly woke at 5am to the sound of her alarm. Far from feeling rested, she felt as though she'd been trampled by imaginary, but very heavy, horses.

Before she did anything else, Holly was going to have a shower.

Heading to the bathroom Holly switched on the water to give it time to heat up. Without even the pretence of intending to condition her hair, Holly raced through a wash and shampoo and then just stood under the gloriously hot water, drawing in the steamy air in great, cleansing breaths. She stayed there far longer than she would usually have allowed herself, only switching the water off when her toes started to prune.

When Holly was little, if she was having an awful day or just couldn't shake a bad mood, her mother would always send her for a shower. She would march her upstairs and into the bathroom telling her, "Wash it away and start fresh.

You'll feel better."

And she was right; Holly always did feel better afterwards. She would dress in clean clothes and brush her hair and enter the day again like a new person, or at least with a new attitude.

Stepping out now onto the bathroom mat, Holly felt lighter. The horrors of the night were washed away and this new, clean Holly was ready for the day. Just without a towel.

Buggar!

Cursing herself for forgetting to fetch a towel from the airing cupboard again, Holly braced herself and then made her mad dash back to her bedroom, grabbing a towel as she passed the door in the hall. The cold air on her wet skin set her shivering and tingling all over and Holly wrapped herself tightly in her large white towel while she dug through her chest of drawers for some clothes for the day. She found some faded blue jeans and a grey top to wear for her deliveries, but opted for a more comfortable pair of black joggers and oversized t-shirt as her morning's baking outfit. Completing the ensemble with a thick pair of cable knit socks bought from the last church fair, she headed to the kitchen and preheated the oven. Checking the fridge and freezer to make sure that there was nothing she'd forgotten, she smiled at the shelves stacked with delicious goodies. Holly had always liked the idea of her baked goods and other food brightening up peoples' days. Cupcakes bought in celebration, muffins consumed for comfort and pastries making a morning feel more manageable. Her people skills may be sub-par, but Holly loved making people happy.

All the chilled food was in order and Holly grabbed a few trays of cookies and transferred them to the oven. For some cafes Holly delivered the food already complete and ready to go, whereas others would receive their orders part-baked or still chilled or frozen, ready to be baked fresh on site. Holly preferred the latter option as it was always nice for people to consume food at its peak, still warm from the oven.

While the cookies baked, Holly turned her attention to the cupcakes. Mentally thanking herself for measuring out all of the ingredients the night before, Holly mixed and added until she had five varieties all ready to go. The traditional vanilla and the double chocolate were the most popular so she had twice as many of these two as she had of the others, but her personal favourite was a biscoff variety. She also had light, buttery lemon cupcakes to be topped with a delicious lemon buttercream, and a chocolate orange flavour that had proved popular during the cooler months but would probably be swapped for a strawberry shortcake or something equally summery very soon.

Grabbing an ice-cream scoop she ladled out even amounts of mixture into dozens and dozens of paper cases, waiting ready in cupcake tins. Sliding these into the oven she then turned her attention to muffins: blueberry crumble, strawberry lemon crumble, raspberry glazed and banana pecan. They were ready to go in the oven just as the cupcakes came out. Holly prised each small cake out of its metal dish and transferred them to cooling racks. While they came to room temperature she whipped up a huge batch of buttercream which she then divided into smaller portions and added the different flavourings. Each was then spooned into piping bags complete with large star nozzles and set in the fridge for just a few minutes to counter the heat of the kitchen. Holly opened the windows to allow some of the accumulated warmth to escape while she carried trays and trays of food down to the van. Once she was left with just the cupcakes to go she set them on their large industrial metal trays and topped each one with a perfect swirl of icing. These were then carried downstairs too and stowed safely on their own shelf in the van. Holly was way ahead of her usual schedule but most of the customers wouldn't mind. She was so regular and dependable normally that a little deviation just this once shouldn't lose her any favour.

The day was beautiful and clear and promised to be warm later. Once her deliveries were all complete Holly would enjoy taking a walk around the perimeter of the woods. If she just so happened to come across a bike that turned out to belong to Terry, so be it.

Before leaving the house Holly grabbed the two boxes of lemon shortbread. She'd need to be careful that they didn't overheat and get too soft, but hopefully her mother would come through with those addresses soon and Holly wanted to be ready when she did.

Chapter 7

The roads were a little quieter so early in the morning and Holly made great time. A few of her customers queried the break from her usual routine and Holly explained about the fundraising dinner. Local customers smiled their understanding and even those further afield in Cambridge understood the appeal a catering job of this scale must hold for her. A few of her stockists even asked if she had business cards for the catering side of the business and Holly agreed to bring some with her on her next delivery. Holly had always been happy with her straightforward day-to-day life, but it had to be said that shaking things up a little and getting out there talking to people was turning out to be great for business!

All deliveries complete, Holly headed back to town. She drove straight to Terry's estate and parked in one of the spaces near the blocks of flats that faced the woods. She didn't feel great about leaving the van for long and the day was warming up quickly, threatening to ruin the lemon shortbread rounds. Holly decided to settle for a brisk walk along the grassy area bordering the trees. If Terry had cycled the two hundred metres to the edge of the woods, this was surely where he would have left his bike. Holly walked the full length of the stretch of grass and then back along it again, weaving in and out of the treeline, in case Terry had manoeuvred his bike into better cover.

Nothing. No sign of a bike. There was always the possibility that the bike had been there to begin with but had been stolen, or possibly the police had recovered Terry's bike and given it back to Kim. Holly was just contemplating heading up to Kim's flat briefly now, when she saw her walking toward her across the flat's car park, not looking particularly thrilled to see Holly.

"Oh, hello" Holly offered awkwardly when Kim reached her.

"I was just on my way home with some milk and I saw you over here walking about." Kim held up the carrier bag she was holding, showing the single pint of semi-skimmed within.

"I was just looking for something," Holly admitted.

Kim didn't ask anything further but looked at Holly levelly, waiting for her to elaborate.

"I was looking for Terry's bike, but maybe you have it?"

Kim looked puzzled. "No, I don't. What do you want his bike for? I asked the police about that actually, it isn't at the flat and I don't know where else it would be." She looked slightly uncomfortable, "I was hoping to sell it. I could probably get a few quid for it and it would help with rent."

Holly couldn't imagine the stress of money troubles on top of losing someone you cared about. Not knowing how you were going to pay your rent each month must be awful. No wonder Kim hadn't asked too many questions about where Terry was getting his money from.

"I was just wondering where it was. I'm not even sure if it's relevant at all to what happened, I just think it's strange that no one's found it. If you can tell me what type it is, I'll know if I come across it and I'll get it back to you," Holly suggested.

"Thanks, that would be good I guess."

Holly made a quick note on her phone of the description of the bike and Kim turned to go. Holly, worried an opportunity like this might be hard to achieve again, called her back.

"Wait! I don't suppose I could ask you a few more questions could I?" she asked tentatively.

"More about drugs I suppose?" Kim was looking defensive but also somehow resigned. Holly wondered if the police had been questioning her. She looked tired.

"No, I don't think so. I just realised how little I asked you before really. Terry was found by my dad on Wednesday morning about 5.30. Did he go out that morning or the night before?"

"Terry up at 5.30?! No chance! It must have been the night before. I was out from about 2pm on the Tuesday and didn't get back until almost 10pm and he'd already gone then. He told me he was working on the Tuesday but he didn't tell me where. He must have gone to the woods after that. I don't know why though. The police think he was doing a drug deal but I think they're idiots."

"Really? Why?"

Kim snorted with amusement. "Well who goes off to the

middle of the woods at night to do a drug deal? It's like a bad TV show."

Holly felt a bit naïve but now that she thought about it, it made sense. What would look more suspicious than two people meeting in the woods in the dark? Much easier to just go to someone's home or meet them by the local corner shop or something. If you seem to be doing something ordinary, it's much less likely to draw attention.

"Where were you on Tuesday from 2pm to 10pm?" It wasn't an easy question to ask but Holly needed to be bold if she was going to find out anything useful.

"I was working at a salon in Cambridge. I rent a chair there on Tuesdays."

"Rent a chair?" Holly was totally ignorant of the beauty world and wasn't really sure how anyone's business besides her own functioned.

"Yeah, I mostly see clients at mine or go to their houses but it's not a big town is it? So a few months ago I started renting a chair on a Tuesday at a salon called 'Sensationail' in Cambridge. I have a few regular clients in Cambridge who come in, but it's mostly walk-ins. It's always busy and I have to get the bus home, so I don't get in until late."

"Would you do my nails?" Holly asked suddenly.

She wasn't really sure where that abrupt question had come from. Now she'd said it she felt silly, she wasn't exactly the nail polish type. But Kim needed money and there was no harm in it, surely. Kim was looking at her as though she knew that this offer was made out of pity and it clearly wasn't appreciated. Holly looked down at her short, uneven nails. She didn't even cut or file them, she just let them break. Her hands were dry and coarse from frequent washing, and calloused from hand mixing. Kim's eyes followed Holly's gaze and widened a little. She smiled slightly. The sight of such a challenge clearly outweighed the disgust she felt at being viewed as a charity case.

"Yeah of course. When would you like?" Kim asked.

They agreed on 7.00 that evening, so that Holly would have time to do all of her baking prep for Saturday beforehand. Holly, thinking of how small her flat was, suggested they do it at her parents' house and maybe her mum could get hers done too. Kim was happy with that and so, plans made, they went their separate ways.

Still no message from her mum, so Holly decided to give her a call.

"Hello darling, how are you?" Maggie asked.

"Hi Mum, I'm fine thanks, I was just wondering if you'd had any luck with those addresses I asked about?" Holly probed.

"Oh yes, I've got them, do you want them now?"

Typical.

"Yes, absolutely! Now would be great!"

Holly dug around in the van door until she found a pen and a clean napkin and she noted them both down.

"Thank you Mum. Just one more thing. How would you like to get your nails done later?" Holly asked in a would-be casual tone.

"I'm sorry? Who is this? This cannot be my darling daughter! This is an imposter! My Holly doesn't believe in

such things as nail varnish!" Maggie exclaimed.
Holly waited for the mocking to subside before she
explained. Her mother was all for it and declared herself to
be 'excited for the pampering.' This left Holly feeling much
more nervous about the whole thing than she had done
before. The term 'pampering' definitely conjured up images
that made Holly feel like a fish out of water.

Chapter 8

Looking at the time Holly judged that she should be able to go and speak to the ladies that Terry had worked for and still have time to prepare her Saturday orders before the looming nail appointment. She checked the addresses that her mother had given her and saw that they were quite close together, near to the town centre.

She was lucky and found space to park just outside Mrs Peters' house. She had an empty driveway but Holly didn't feel comfortable parking there without permission, and she didn't want to make an elderly woman feel pressured to talk to her or answer questions if she wasn't comfortable with it. Grabbing the canvas bag that she had stowed the boxes of lemon shortbread in, Holly headed up the driveway of the small house on foot. The front garden was lovely, with evidence of bulbs erupting all along the flowerbeds. Some late tulips and daffodils were still in attendance, and Holly saw salvia, irises and many other beautiful flowers that she couldn't name. Reaching the house, she knocked on a pale yellow door and it was soon opened by an old lady who was so perfect as to almost be a caricature. A hand-knitted pink cardigan was buttoned over a floral dress with a white lace collar. She had neat white curls with a faint blue rinse that served to accentuate the pale blue eyes that had probably had more of a sapphire hue in her youth. She was very small, probably no more than five feet, and she was smiling warmly up at Holly. She could have walked right out of the pages of a fairy tale. Holly suppressed the urge to look around her for sinister, lurking wolves.

"Hello dear? Can I help you?" Mrs Peters asked her.

Even her voice was perfect. She was the quintessential little old lady.

"Hello, my name is Holly, I believe you know my mother from church. I'm Maggie Abbot's daughter." Holly felt massively relieved to have this opening, it wasn't easy to just turn up at a strangers house!

"Oh of course! Maggie! I do hope she's alright?"

"Oh she's absolutely fine! It was actually something else that I was hoping to talk to you about. And I brought you some lemon shortbread."

Holly held up one of the boxes in offering and was immediately ushered inside.

Within moments she had been settled in a pink brocade armchair in a pink living room. The biscuits had been transferred to a willow pattern plate, and Holly and Mrs Peters each held a saucer and matching teacup of very sweet, very milky tea.

"Call me Gladys dear. Now what was it that you wanted to speak to me about?" she asked politely.

"It's about someone that you know. Unfortunately they've passed away." Holly regretted not planning beforehand what she was going to say. Her words felt clumsy and she wasn't sure how straightforward to be.

"Ah, oh dear. Who is it now then?"

Seeing Holly's expression, Gladys looked sweetly sympathetic and explained,

"I'm afraid that once you reach a certain age dear, it begins to seem as though all of one's acquaintance are just falling away around one."

She seemed to be at peace with this state of affairs so Holly pressed on.

"It's Terry Wood. I think he worked for you?"

At this Gladys' face fell.

"Oh. He was young. I can't say that I was particularly fond of the boy but it's never nice to lose the young ones." Gladys commented in a sombre tone.

"You weren't fond of him? Do you mind if I ask why?" Holly queried.

"One should never speak ill of the dead. May I ask what happened to him?" Gladys asked her.

"I'm afraid he was murdered." Holly admitted.

"Good gracious! You don't really think of things like that happening do you? Not to people that you know." She looked sad and thoughtful now. Holly didn't speak immediately, hoping to think of a way round 'not speaking ill of the dead'.

"No, it's definitely shocking. I've been trying to find some reason why this might have happened."

Holly looked at her hopefully but Gladys wasn't taking the bait.

"There's no rhyme or reason for the evils men do."

Not particularly useful. If Gladys was right it was going to be very difficult to discover who had perpetrated this particular evil. Holly mumbled something non-committal about supposing that this were true and looked about her for some way to keep the conversation going in the right direction without Gladys shutting her down. The room was immaculate, there was not a speck of dust and everything looked perfectly placed.

"What did Terry do for you? I understand that he did cleaning for a lot of jobs," Holly probed.

"Yes, he did a spot of dusting around the place and ran the hoover round. He was supposed to help in the garden too but apparently he wasn't the outdoors type. It was just temporary, after I had surgery on my hip. It was difficult for me to get around and the house was a bit much for me to manage. He hasn't worked for me for a few weeks though. I had a word with Joe and he took care of that for me."

"Joe Dawkins?" Holly asked.

"Yes, dear Joe, he's usually such a help! It's a shame but never mind," Gladys uttered cryptically.

"Why was it a shame? Because things didn't work out with Terry?"

"Anyone can be mistaken in someone's character." Gladys' tone was stern. She pursed her lips and clearly wasn't willing to talk any further about any of Terry's possible shortcomings.

"When did you last see Terry?" Holly asked, feeling that this at least must be a safe question.

"Just over three weeks ago I think. Yes, he was here on the Friday that week but then I spoke to Joe after church and Terry hasn't been here again," Gladys told her.

"He didn't happen to leave his bike here did he?" Holly asked.

"That bicycle of his? No dear, I haven't seen it since I saw him. It wasn't stolen was it?" Gladys asked quickly.

"What makes you say that?"

"Oh nothing really." Gladys pursed her lips again.

"Was Terry stealing? Was that why you asked Joe to stop him from coming?" Holly pressed.

"I'm sure I can't say, I think it's time you left dear, I'm sorry but I'm very busy today. Do say hello to your mother for me won't you? Dear Maggie, such a lovely lady."

And just like that Holly found herself back outside the pale yellow door, feeling that she hadn't really gained much at all. If Terry had been stealing from Gladys that would certainly be interesting, but Gladys hadn't confirmed that that was the case so Holly wasn't really sure where to go with the idea. She supposed that she could ask Joe Dawkins about it. If Gladys had enlisted his help in firing Terry then he was likely to know the reason behind it. Holly was surprised that Joe had still spoken positively about Terry if he had indeed been stealing from a little old lady while she recovered from surgery. Really, the more Holly found out about his character, the less she mourned his loss.

Holly checked the second address again and decided that as it was such a beautiful day and only a few minutes to the second house, she would go on foot.

Chapter 9

The streets were all lined with small houses with beautiful front gardens. This was one of the oldest areas of town and many of the residents had been in these homes since they were in their twenties. Families had been started here, raised here and children had grown and moved on. Now the parents remained, many turned into grandparents or even great grandparents, but still in their first homes. Holly passed many elderly couples tending their flowers together or sitting out on garden chairs reading their newspapers. It struck Holly as a beautiful way to live. Only a couple of the houses appeared to have gone through a change of ownership, their gardens now had bright plastic slides or wooden Wendy houses. Their flower beds were not quite so neat and manicured, as work and child raising didn't leave much time for gardening.

Holly's destination was a small brick house. The paint around the windows was chipped and the windows themselves needed cleaning. The front garden had the appearance of neglect but Holly could see that over the years bulbs and perennials had been planted, so it must once have been cared for. The door was a faded blue and also in need of a new coat of paint as chips flaked off when Holly knocked. It took a long time and a couple of subsequent raps of the knuckle for the door to be opened but finally another elderly woman stood before her. Mrs Weiss was just as stereotypical as Gladys in her way, but they appeared so different as to be practically different species. Where Gladys was small and delicate, this woman's diminished size gave the impression of a conservation of power, like a coiled spring. Where Gladys' face had been smiling and open, this woman's was sharp and suspicious. Here was another floral dress and another cardigan, and yet on this woman it somehow looked like a uniform chosen for status and practicality, rather than for aesthetics.

"What do you want? I'm not buying anything," she barked.

"No, I'm not selling anything!" Holly hastened to reassure her, though Mrs Weiss didn't look particularly reassured at all, rather her look of suspicion deepened.

"Then why are you here? Who are you?" the small woman demanded.

"My name is Holly, I think you know my mother, Maggie Abbot, from church. I wanted to talk to you for a minute." She trailed off uncertainly under a steely gaze, "I brought you biscuits."

After a moment's hesitation, Mrs Weiss held out a hand. "Let me try one."

She remained where she was, blocking the doorway and waited to be presented with a biscuit. This wasn't a promising start but Holly couldn't help but smile at the slightly outrageous behaviour. She opened the box of shortbread and placed one in the woman's palm. It was held up and examined by a pair of dark grey, intelligent eyes. She sniffed it gently before taking a bite, her eyes widening a little.

"Good crumble. And the butter and lemon balance is good too. You don't use a lemon extract do you?" she asked.

"No," Holly responded surprised "A little of my own lemon curd in the mixture and lots of juice and zest. I use good lemons too, that's important."

"I know that's important! Not easy to do now though. I make my own lemon bars and they used to be wonderful. Now all you can get in the shops is these puny, waxed things. And the markets are all just cast-offs from the supermarkets these days." She looked at Holly accusingly as though she personally were responsible for the decline of available produce.

"I get mine from a good supplier. I have a bakery company. Sorry."

The woman smirked slightly at the apology but finally stood aside and let Holly in. Given the state of its exterior, Holly had been expecting the house to be rundown and uncared for but in fact it was very clearly loved. Even the baseboards showed no signs of dust and the walls were covered in pictures and photographs, all perfectly clean. There were paintings of flowers and countless photos of people that Holly could see were Mrs Weiss' family. There were baby photos and wedding photos and more candid pictures of people sat around in gardens or grouped on sofas or playing on the beach. The further they moved into the house the more loved and cared for it seemed to be. Paintings by enthusiastic toddlers now graced the walls, most of them lovingly placed in frames.

Every surface was filled with knick-knacks or thriving plants. Holly couldn't keep a single potted plant alive to save her own life, let alone this many!

They proceeded through to a very colourful and respectably proportioned kitchen and Mrs Weiss fetched a bottle of cream soda from the fridge and two glasses before leading Holly out onto a patio in the most beautiful back garden Holly had ever seen. She looked around her in wonder at peonies with flowers the size of dinner plates, pink and blue hydrangeas, scarlet camellias with so much colour you could barely make out glimpses of leaves. There were tulips in every colour and great bushes of lilac. It wasn't neat or orderly, but everything was clearly being tended to reach its fullest potential. Plants spilled over one another and flowers reached up through unrelated bushes. Wherever things had sprouted, they had been encouraged to grow. Holly loved it.

Mrs Weiss had already pulled out a chair from a matching wrought iron table and sat down. She was now looking back at Holly, frozen in place in the doorway, with an amused yet appreciative smile. Holly shook herself and moved forward to join her host.

"It isn't what I expected. The front garden was nice enough but this... this is wonderful." Holly told her sincerely.

The woman was really smiling now, a proper smile that

transformed her face. Holly caught a glimpse of a beautiful young woman shining through.

"All those people doing up their front gardens, they're just show-boating! That's what they're doing! Showing off! But this is my space." She smiled around her "This is where my great grandchildren play. My Walter and I put this garden together for our family"

"Walter's your husband?" Holly asked.

"He was. I married Walter when I was nineteen. How old are you?" Mrs Weiss asked, her voice ominous and her eyes narrowed.

"Older than nineteen," Holly admitted.

"Are you married?" the older woman barked.

"No," Holly confessed.

"You said you have a bakery company. A career. I suppose that's no bad thing these days, it seems to be what people do." She said it was no bad thing, but Holly didn't think that it would have been possible to look more disapproving.

"I'm very happy Mrs Weiss," Holly hastened to assure her. Seeing the look of impatience and disbelief that her words were met with, she rushed on,

"I'm not saying I won't get married one day, it's just not something that I expect to be doing any time soon." She was flustered at the unexpected turn of the conversation and she knew that her discomfort was painfully apparent but her companion looked in no way embarrassed by it, if anything she looked quite pleased.

"Call me Rebecca," she told her, reaching into the box

and taking another of the lemon shortbreads and smiling tenderly at it before consuming it in two slow bites.

"So, Gladys tells me that you want to ask about Terry Wood?" Rebecca queried calmly.

"Sorry?" Holly asked, confused.

"Terry Wood. The good-for-nothing Joe told me could help me out around the house. What did you want to know?"

"Gladys called you?" Holly asked.

"Of course she did dear. Women living alone, we look out for each other," Rebecca informed her in a condescending tone.

That meant that when Rebecca had left her standing on the front porch and pretended to think she was a salesperson of some kind, she'd already known exactly who Holly was, Gladys had already filled her in. Holly wasn't sure whether to be annoyed or amused as she looked at the smiling woman before her. Rebecca certainly seemed to enjoy getting the upper hand.

"Ok, you said that Terry was a good-   for-nothing, what do you mean by that?" Holly asked her.

"I mean that from the first time he stepped foot in this house it was clear that he was nothing but trouble. He was no help whatsoever. He seemed to think that just because I'm old I wouldn't notice that he wasn't cleaning when he said he was. He would show up late, do nothing at all and expect to be paid for his time. I like Joe so I put up with it for a while but when money started going missing I'd had enough."

"So he was stealing? You're sure?" Holly asked quickly.

Rebecca looked disappointed to find her so naïve.

"Yes, he was stealing. I don't know what Joe was thinking, he always seemed like a sensible enough man before, but how he could vouch for that boy I'll never understand," Rebecca told her, shaking her head sadly.

"When was this? When did you last see Terry?" Holly queried.

"This was about four weeks ago now. I told Joe I didn't want him anywhere near my house again and then I told Gladys to do the same."

"Was he stealing from her too?" Holly asked.

"Oh yes. He took a fair amount of cash from her and she even found him searching through her bedroom once, no doubt looking for jewellery. Not that Gladys' husband had ever been one for buying her baubles and nice things," Rebecca recounted, her tone bitter.

Holly looked at her inquisitively.

"Not a nice man. You saw her house? All that pink? We painted it the week after he died, in celebration. I even bought champagne to mark the occasion," Rebecca told her with a delighted cackle. She smiled at the memory but Holly was shocked. She hadn't much experience of unhappy marriages and Gladys' prim good manners wouldn't have led Holly to suspect such a thing about her. She wasn't sure what to say.

"It looks nice pink," she offered feebly.

Rebecca gave a bark of laughter.

"Not my colour, but Gladys loves it and that's all that matters in the end. But I shouldn't gossip. Gladys would hate me talking about her. What more did you want to know about Terry?" Rebecca asked her tone brisk and businesslike now.

"Did he leave a bicycle here?" Holly asked her.

"Well that's an odd question, but no. No he didn't. He rode one when he came here but he always took it away with him again," Rebecca assured her.

"Have you seen Terry since he stopped working here?" Holly asked, keen to keep the conversation focused on Terry rather than her own private life.

"No, he doesn't attend church and I've not run into him anywhere else," Rebecca told her simply.

"Do you know of anyone Terry was having problems with?" Holly asked.

"No, I wasn't well enough acquainted with him for that. Mind, I can't think that anyone who knew him wouldn't have had problems with him. Now one for you," Rebecca leant forwards in her chair, watching Holly intently.

"Sorry?" Holly asked her, puzzled.

"It's your turn to answer a question. Why are you here asking me all this?" Rebecca asked her with evident interest.

"I'm sorry?" Holly queried, buying herself time.

"You're a baker, yes? Not a police officer? So why are you here?" Rebecca demanded.

Holly took a deep breath. It was a good question but it was surprisingly difficult to answer. She knew why she had started looking into things, but it had already become so much more complicated. The more people she had spoken to, the more it became clear that the police weren't exactly going to be lacking in suspects. So why was she still investigating?

"I started looking into it because my dad was the one who discovered Terry's body. They didn't get on when my dad taught him in school and I was worried that the police would think that he did it. Then, once I'd started I couldn't stop. If I just stopped investigating it would be like saying that it didn't matter after all. Someone's dead. That should always matter." Holly explained clumsily, willing Rebecca to understand.

Rebecca gave her a clear, assessing look.

"That's good. You're capable. And more importantly, you know you're capable. I like to see a young lady step up and get things done. It's good to be independent like that. I'd like you to meet my grandson," she told Holly, sitting back with a satisfied smile.

This abrupt change in the conversation wasn't what Holly had been expecting. Instinctively she laughed, though she didn't think her companion was joking.

"How can you say that it's good to be independent and then try to fix me up with someone?" she asked chuckling.

Rebecca looked a little puzzled now.

"My dear, why on earth should being in a relationship take away your independence? It's always better to have love."

She stated it quite simply, with an affectionate smile and Holly noted that she was a world away from the cantankerous old lady who had first opened the door. Holly was beginning to suspect that the grumpy old lady bit had all been an act for Rebecca's own amusement and that she would in fact be a wonderful friend.

"Well maybe I'll meet him some day, but no promises," Holly offered as a compromise.

Rebecca gave another bark of laughter.

"That's right girl! Play hard to get!"

Still chuckling, she reached for another lemon shortbread while Holly poured them each a glass of the cream soda. Sitting comfortably with her cold, sweet drink, looking out over the flowers, Holly wondered if she would have a home with a garden of its own one day. It had always been the vague plan but Holly wasn't exactly taking any steps in that direction. Maybe Kat was right and she should be getting out and socialising more. For now though, just this was nice. Holly stayed for another hour talking with Rebecca about recipes and family and how to grow the perfect rose bush. When she did leave, it was only after an exchange of telephone numbers and a promise of further acquaintance.

Chapter 10

Holly had to admit that the investigation had stalled. Her plans for the rest of the day however, were very clear. Holly had a few hours to get all of the orders for Saturday ready and then she needed to head over to her parents' house in time for her nail appointment that evening with Kim. She headed home and took a moment to look around her small flat. In contrast with Rebecca's house, it barely looked lived in. There were no photos or pictures on the walls, no rugs or potted plants and she hadn't even painted since moving in. Every room was the same neutral eggshell as the day she had first set foot inside. Her brother Rob had once remarked that she'd moved out of their parents' house but she'd never really moved in here. Maybe when she got a free day, Holly would look at some paint colours. For now though, she needed to get baking.

Saturday orders meant scones. This was good news as they could be baked in advance and warmed up for sale. Holly worked the butter, sugar and flour together with a pastry cutter until she had a breadcrumb like mixture. Then she stirred in buttermilk to create a sticky, floury, wet mess.

She turned this out onto a heavily floured work surface and beneath her hands it transformed into perfect scone batter. She made dark chocolate and raspberry, blueberry and lemon and a batch of traditional raisin. Cutting out inch thick zig-zag rounds she transferred them onto baking trays and then it was into the oven.

Next up was cookies and she had all of her usual flavours whipped up in what felt like no time. She doubled up on the chocolate varieties as people seemed to be more likely to treat themselves at the weekend and her customers' order sizes reflected this.

Next she assembled paninis. Sun-dried tomato and a local cheddar was a popular one. The standard 'ham and cheese' was probably the only one that beat it for numbers. Holly much preferred the brie with sliced pear, but people weren't always as adventurous with their orders as she would like. Once she'd developed some more healthy food options for Jack to sell at the leisure centre, maybe she could develop some more panini fillings. It was always nice to come up with a flavour combination that really made a toasted sandwich into a treat. Maybe she could make something summery and entice people to be a bit more daring in their food choices.

Lastly Holly measured out all of the ingredients for her cupcakes and muffins again, and covered the bowls to await her early morning preparations. Checking her watch Holly saw that it was just gone six. If she ate some dinner here she might be late getting to the nail appointment. With a sigh she pulled out her phone and called her mother.

"Hey, Mum?"

"You are not cancelling the nail appointment! I'm looking forward to it!"

"I'm not cancelling, don't worry."

"Oh OK, in that case darling, what's up?"

"I was wondering if I could have dinner with you tonight? I'm worried I'll be late if I cook something here and I've got the kitchen all ready for tomorrow morning."

"No problem, it's just pesto pasta but you're welcome to join us. I've just got the water boiling now, it'll be ready in about fifteen minutes."

"Ok amazing, I'll just get changed and head straight over. I don't need to wear anything special do I? For a nail appointment I mean."

"Why darling, do you own something special?"

Her mother was teasing but they both knew that Holly actually didn't own anything special. Her wardrobe ranged from joggers to jeans and that was it. On this occasion Holly opted for darker blue jeans and another grey t-shirt. Hopefully this would be fine for whatever Kim needed to do.

She set off for her parents' house, wondering if it was too late to call Kim and cancel after all. She knew that she was being silly to be so scared, it was just a manicure, but not knowing what to expect had always made Holly nervous.

Her mother's face when she answered the door was enough to banish any thoughts of cancelling. Maggie was bubbling with excitement. She led Holly though to the dining room where dinner was ready on the table. Her father was already seated and gave her a teasing smile.

"A nail appointment? Are you feeling ok?"

Oddly this opposition made her feel more confident.

"I can get my nails done! It's not so crazy!"

"Exactly!" Maggie strode back into the room with bread in one hand and butter in the other. "Every lady deserves to do something nice for herself every once in a while. I think I'll go for a red. Or maybe a pink. But magenta, something really bright! I haven't had my nails done in years now! I used to go to a salon sometimes when you kids were young but it's been aeons now! I never thought we'd be doing something like this together!"

She beamed across at her daughter and for the first time Holly wondered if her mother would have liked a more girly daughter. Wanting to play with her brothers meant that Holly had cast aside dresses and ballet in favour of dungarees and climbing trees. As she got older she had never experimented with make-up, never borrowed her mother's high heels. After three sons, Maggie might have been clamouring to raise a princess.

"Well if it goes alright and the nails don't get in the way of baking, maybe we could make this a regular thing."

Maggie's smile was infectious. Holly couldn't help but grin back at the look of excitement on her mother's face.

"I'm going to open a bottle of wine!" her mother cried happily.

As Maggie bounced up from the table Holly's phone buzzed in her pocket. She fished it out and looked at the screen.

"It's Kat." As she answered and held the phone to her

ear her mother stuck her head back around the kitchen door and mouthed, "Invite her! Girls' night!!"

"Hi Kat, what's up?" Holly asked.

"I'm bored. What are you up to? Do you want to do a movie night or something?"

"Um, I can't I'm actually busy this evening."

"A date?!" Kat asked hopefully.

"No! I'm... I'm getting my nails done," Holly admitted.

"What?!" Kat practically shrieked the word. Next to her, Holly's father jumped.

Holly sighed. "Kim's coming round to my parents' house at seven. Can you get here by then?"

"Are you kidding?! I'm leaving right now!"

With that she hung up and Holly put down her phone, amused and exasperated in equal measure. Had she really become so set in her ways that getting her nails done was this much of a shock to everyone?

Her mother danced back into the room clutching a bottle of white wine and two glasses. She poured one out for Holly and one for herself. Richard gave a theatrical splutter of surprise which was met with a stern look.

"This is a girls' night. The men don't get wine on girls' night. Besides, you'll need to drive Holly home later, she *is* drinking," Maggie informed her husband matter-of-factly.

Kat rang the doorbell at ten minutes to seven, just as Holly and her mother were stacking their freshly washed plates on the draining rack. She whirled in, in a cloud of perfume and enthusiasm, blonde hair bouncing with every delighted step.

"Girl's night!"

She hadn't stopped to change and was wearing leggings and a t-shirt, but Holly couldn't help noting that on Kat it looked relaxed and chic whereas she suspected that if she donned a similar outfit it would just look lumpy and plain. Kat held a full bottle of white wine aloft and she looked just as thrilled as Maggie. However this evening went, Holly decided it was worth it to see two of her favourite people so happy. Besides, who knew how many evenings like this she and Kat would have time for?

Kat's wine was stashed in the fridge to stay cool and Maggie poured them each a glass from the bottle still open from dinner. They sat around the table and discussed colours while they waited for Kim. Kat had just announced that she was going to have 'Ruby Slipper' which was her absolute favourite, when the doorbell rang. A moment later Richard led Kim in, laden with bags. Kat stood up and gave Kim a brief hug.

"Hiya! Is it OK if I join? I couldn't miss out on Holly's first time!"

Kim chuckled. "Of course. Just let me get set up."

She unzipped one of the bags and took out a strange contraption that Holly didn't recognise and some bottles of a clear liquid that Holly didn't trust. Next came cotton buds, and pieces of gauze and a range of nail files and other, more threatening, looking implements. Once she'd pulled out a large bottle of hand lotion and some latex gloves, the first bag was empty. The second bag contained nail polish. Holly had no idea that there were so many colours! Seeing them all laid out like that, they were beautiful, but it was the names that captured Holly. They had the most captivating names and Holly had no idea how to choose among them! Ruby Slipper was too... red. Midnight Rendezvous was beautiful but maybe too dark. It was a deep, inky indigo with a faint sparkle to it. Buttercream Delight was very tempting. It was a pale yellow and beautifully summery. Maggie chose Flamingo Dancing, a bright, perfect pink. With so many options, Holly was completely lost.

"I tell you what, I'll do Kat's first and then you Maggie, and then Holly, so you've got time to decide what you want to have. You'll be able to watch and see what happens too, so you'll know what to expect."

Holly watched closely as Kat's nails were painted a brilliant red and the polish set between coats with a sort of UV contraption. Kim explained that if she looked after them she could get through three weeks without them chipping. She'd need to wear rubber gloves when washing up, but Holly almost always did so anyway, otherwise her hands would be in an even worse state than they were. Under Kim's careful ministrations, Kat's nails and then Maggie's were coated in a beautiful colour. All the while Holly sat holding a whole reel of test samples, all in different delicate shades of nude. She was tempted by a neutral looking taupe colour called 'Soundless Whisper'.

The second bottle of wine was fetched and Holly admitted to herself that it felt nice to have all of them sat around together drinking and chatting. They teased Holly gently about her lack of dating. They asked Kat questions about Dan that got only coyly evasive answers. They listened to Maggie complaining affectionately about Holly's dad, and they all renewed their sympathies to Kim.

She sighed, "To be honest, I'm probably better off. If I could have afforded the rent on my own I think I would have been rid of him way back," Kim admitted.

"What will you do about rent love?" It was a difficult question to ask but Maggie never shied away from difficult. She always said you should ask the hard questions, it makes it easier for people to ask for help if they need it.

"My dad's sending me some money. He's going to help me out for a bit, just until I can get some more work together. It's just difficult building up enough regulars to know that you're going to be alright month to month," Kim explained.

"Do you have business cards?" Holly asked her.

"No, I mean... I just do nails, it's not really a business is it," Kim mumbled, a flush creeping up her neck.

"Of course it is. I just bake, but that doesn't mean it's not my business. You have to take yourself seriously. Get some business cards printed and I'll ask in the cafes I deliver to if I can leave some on the counter for people to take," Holly told her.

"I'll take some for church!" Maggie chimed in, "I bet lots of the ladies would love to get their nails done and if you could go to them, all the better!"

Kim was looking tentatively excited now, like someone who was naturally hopeful but had had too many knock backs to really trust it.

"You really think so?" she asked them?

"Definitely." Kat's tone was absolutely sure and certain. She looked down at her perfect, glossy nails. "You're really good at this Kim."

"Alright, as soon as my dad sends the money I'll get some business cards made. Thanks."

She smiled around at them and happily resumed the finishing touches of Maggie's nails. Turning to Holly she saw the sample reel in her hands and sighed like an exasperated parent with a tired toddler. She eased the reel out of Holly protesting hands, looked about her and picked up another, much brighter reel of colours.

"Ok, choose from these colours. Don't overthink it, just pick whichever one you think is the prettiest," Kim told her.

Holly looked at them.

"That one."

"Ok, that one it is." Kim responded with a smile.

"What?! I can't have that one! It won't suit me! I need something less obvious," Holly argued.

Kim looked at her, smiling understandingly.

"It's alright to pick something fun Holly. They're just nails."

It was just once,.. she could pick something more subdued next time. The name clinched it. It was called 'Enchanted Garden.' Holly allowed herself to be persuaded.

And so, Holly's hands were transformed. The calluses couldn't be totally removed, and the dry skin was a work in progress, but for now Holly's hands were soft and (mostly) smooth. Her uneven, broken nails were all filed into even, uniform ovals. These ovals were then painted a beautiful, bright lilac with iridescent sparkles. Looking at her fingers, Holly felt... pretty. It was probably the wine.

Either way, she promised that they would repeat the evening once a month and she already knew that she wasn't going to be picking something subdued. Now that she'd seen how lovely the colours looked, Holly wasn't going to be able to settle for something dull. Maybe next time she'd see if there was a coral colour? That might be nice for summer...

Kim hadn't been drinking so she drove Kat and then herself home. Holly would have loved to sleep at her parents' house again but she had an early start in the morning. Her dad agreed to drive her home in her van and then get a taxi home himself. It wasn't a perfect plan but Holly and her vehicle both needed to be at her own flat at 5am so they agreed that this was the best option any of them could think of.

Once her dad had told her how pretty her nails looked, they passed most of the drive in comfortable silence; as they neared Holly's flat however, it became clear that Richard wanted to say something. He kept glancing over at her and a few times he seemed to be about to speak.

"Dad, what is it?" Holly asked eventually.

"You will be careful won't you?" he asked her gently.

"What?"

"I worry enough about Dan as it is, I don't want to have to worry about you too," he told her.

"Ah."

"Yes. Quite. I'm not going to tell you stop; you're an

adult, you make your own choices, but please just be careful."

"So mum told you I'm looking into Terry? I'm not doing anything dangerous, I promise," she assured her father.

"I don't think that it occurred to your mum that it even *could* be dangerous. All these crime shows you both watch, I think the whole thing has started to feel unreal to you. But someone real killed Terence Wood. They hit him in the head with a rock. Even if you're just talking to people, you could be making yourself a target, or you could even go and talk to the killer without knowing!"

Holly didn't know what to say. She knew how real this was, that was why she was doing this, but she had to admit that she hadn't fully thought through the possible implications. Was she making herself a target? She'd pretty much spent her life trying not to be noticed and now here she was potentially making herself stand out to a murderer.

"I'll be careful dad, I promise."

"Don't talk to anyone alone. Stick to public places or have someone with you. If you don't feel safe in a situation, don't tell yourself you're overreacting or just being silly, just get out. Don't be afraid to run," he told her, his tone as serious as she'd ever heard it.

She looked into the eyes of her wonderful, sincere, fiercely protective father.

"I promise."

Chapter 11

Holly waited for the taxi with her father and then went up to her flat. Her mind was running very fast after their talk and she could feel futile adrenaline coursing through her veins. She got ready for bed but sleep felt impossible. She went into the hall and found her bag, digging through it until she unearthed the menu for tomorrow's event. Taking it to bed with her she decided to run though her plans for the meal to help calm her racing brain. The next most soothing thing to cooking, was thinking about cooking. The menu and list of purchased ingredients were both very crumpled, like they'd been shoved into Joe's desk drawer very quickly. Holly didn't understand how anyone could keep their work space in such disorder. If she did so in the kitchen it could be catastrophic!

Smoothing out the paper, Holly started to read.

It wasn't a complex meal but there was scope for Holly to make it her own. There was a starter of summer salad which would be covered in Holly's perfect salad dressing. The main course was a lasagne, one meat and one smaller vegetarian variety. With spring greens and asparagus on the side, this would be lovely. Lasagne was always a rich, comforting dish but Holly knew how to elevate it to something really special. It was also easier to bake one large tray of lasagne and cut it up, rather than dozens of small individual dishes, especially when you didn't know what the serving arrangements were. They would probably have tins and roasting trays and pots etc. there for her to use but Holly planned to take her own anyway. She looked at the numbers of guests and she calculated that she had a tray just the right size for the meat lasagne. Dessert was always the main event at a dinner like this and Holly was pleased to see that it was something fun. Mini pavlovas. Holly could see that there was cream and assorted fruit on the supplies list, to top some home-made meringue, but she had her own ideas on that front.

Holly finally drifted off to sleep, not to dream of murder and misdeeds, but instead to dream of béchamel sauce and thick tomato passatta.

At five am Holly was woken by her alarm. Pushing her hair out of her face, she caught sight of her nails and smiled. It was a good start to the morning. She lay for a moment enjoying the feeling of excitement bubbling in her chest at the day that lay before her, then she headed for the bathroom. She'd done almost all of her food preparation the day before and she'd gotten up a little early too. She was going to treat herself. Standing under the hot water she took her time, shampooing and conditioning her hair and just relaxing and washing away any lingering traces of tiredness from the wine the night before. She stepped out onto the mat.

Argh! That stupid towel! Never mind, it wasn't going to

spoil her morning. Holly darted and grabbed a towel on the way back to her bedroom. She fished out joggers and a t-shirt to do her initial baking in, but chose a nice pair of jeans and a light blue t-shirt to wear afterwards. Maybe she could ask Kat to go shopping with her soon. It wouldn't hurt to have some nicer clothes. Smiling at the thought she set off for the kitchen.

The cupcakes and muffins were all whipped up and in the oven in no time at all and Holly even had time to sit down and eat a couple of slices of toast and drink a cup of tea. Despite her life revolving around food, Holly's meals tended to be somewhat sporadic. She now took a moment to enjoy the feeling of having things under control. She munched on toast with peanut butter and raspberry jam, sipped at her tea and read through the menu and ingredients list again. After washing up her mug and plate she grabbed a canvas bag and started filling it with a few things that she wanted to take with her to the youth centre to use for the dinner. She grabbed some fresh thyme, some cloves, some peppercorns, her good salt, a small pot of dijon mustard, a few blocks of dark chocolate, golden syrup, her piping bags and nozzles and some cinnamon. She put this bag on the counter and then pulled out her big roasting tin for the lasagne. She filled this with pots, pans, her knives, a garlic crusher and some other bits and bobs. She wouldn't take this with her yet, one of her produce deliveries came on a Saturday and she would need to swing by the flat and sign for it after she had completed her deliveries. Then she could grab everything that she needed before heading over to the youth centre. Hopefully this would give her time to think of anything that she'd forgotten.

Her deliveries all went smoothly and Holly even enjoyed chatting with some of her customers while they set up for the day. She had felt different recently, bolder and more open. She supposed it was a result of pushing herself out of her usual comfort zone. Perhaps she was maturing and shedding some of her social ineptitude, she mused. All deliveries complete, she headed back to her flat and was just in time to see the truck pull in ahead of her. She bounced out of her van and saw the driver do a double take, probably not used so seeing her so happy and energised. She walked over to him and smiled.

"Good morning!"

He smiled back, a big, slightly goofy grin.

"Hey there! How are you this morning?" he asked.

"Good, thanks, I'll just run this stuff upstairs and bring your crates back, give me two minutes," she told him.

"That's ok, no worries, want me to give you a hand? It's no trouble!" he offered.

Holly hesitated for a moment; the driver had never offered to help her carry her order before, but to be honest she wasn't even sure if it was the same guy or not.

"No that's ok, thank you though," she assured him.

Remembering her promise to her father Holly grabbed the crates herself and rushed upstairs with them, stumbling slightly under the weight. Once she reached her flat she moved everything as quickly as she could onto the kitchen counters and hefting the empty crates, much more easily, she headed back down. She signed for the delivery and went to go back up, but the driver detained her.

"So, you got fun plans today?"

"Sorry?"

"You know, you got anything nice planned? For... today...?" he finished somewhat lamely. It took Holly a moment to realise that he was flirting with her. She had watched guys fall apart like this around Kat for years, but never with her!

"Oh!" She smiled sympathetically, "I'm working. I have a catering job later. I have to go." She tried to look kind but not too kind whilst exiting the situation as quickly as possible.

"Alright! Bye then!" he called after her. She turned and waved briefly before heading back indoors and closing the door behind her with relief. She looked down at her sparkly lilac nails accusingly.

"This is all your fault!"

Holly headed upstairs and transferred the chilled foods to the fridge and the flours and sugars to the cupboards. She set aside half a dozen beautiful looking lemons in a paper bag to drop round to Rebecca. Since they'd talked about it previously she thought it would be a nice gesture, and she liked the old lady, she'd be pleased to keep her in her life. Holly chuckled to herself, Kat was always telling her to put herself out there and make more friends but somehow Holly didn't think that Rebecca was quite what she had in mind.

Holly grabbed her canvas bag and the stack of trays and pots that she'd assembled earlier and headed back out to the van. It was still early, only just coming up to half eight and Holly couldn't be sure that Rebecca would be up yet. She decided just to leave the bag of lemons next to the front door and hope that Rebecca would see them. At the very least she would likely be going to church the following day and would find them then. The lemons were perfect and fresh, they could survive a day if they needed to. However, Holly made a mental note that if she had time she'd give Rebecca a quick call later and check that she'd got them.

Now it was off to the youth centre. Holly wanted to get there to help Joe with the food delivery, she just hoped it wasn't the same driver...

She needn't have worried; the driver was a brunette woman in her forties who didn't seem at all inclined to flirt with her. She might have engaged in a little verbal dalliance with Joe given half the chance, but his cheerful efficiency didn't leave room for it. One thing that you could say about Joe, he got the job done. They had all the food into the kitchen and laid out on the surfaces in a matter of minutes. Joe laughed good-naturedly when he saw that she'd brought her own cookware with her and once he was sure that she was settled and knew how to work the oven he excused himself on the grounds of being a terrible cook. Holly didn't mind, now that she had the ingredients in front of her she was happy to crack on. Holly loved baking, she really did, but it was wonderful putting together meals like this. A full three course dinner allowed her the scope to be really creative. Being able to cover the savoury and the sweet and to feed people until they were really satiated was a gift that didn't come around often and Holly savoured it. It would have been nice to be able to create her own menu of course, but really, working with someone else's was its own kind of challenge.

Once the meat and other chilled ingredients had been transferred to the fridge Holly was ready to get to work. She smiled and hummed to herself as she started finely chopping onions and adding them to a large pan. Carrots, peppers and courgettes went the same way. Dozens of tomatoes were peeled and chopped before joining the food already starting to sizzle slightly on the hob. A little good quality vegetable stock and a few bay leaves were added and then it was set to simmer until everything was cooked and the liquid had reduced down. A few large aubergines were sliced, oiled and salted and placed in the oven to roast.

Now for the pasta sheets. It was fiddly to make your own pasta but Holly felt that it was worth it. Using boxed lasagne sheets when she was being paid to prepare a meal would feel like cheating. She may as well get them each a ready meal from Tesco! Once the sheets were rolled out to the correct thickness she laid them between layers of baking parchments and put them in a sealed glass container to stay fresh. Next up would be the white sauce; this was what really set Holly's lasagne apart from others. Before she made the béchamel she poured her milk into a pan. She added a quartered onion, and a few whole garlic cloves, some peppercorns, bay leaves, cloves and a tiny grating of nutmeg. She allowed this to simmer on a low heat until the flavours infused with the milk and then she strained the milk into a large jug. Now she made a basic roux and started to add her flavoured milk concoction. This created a white sauce full of delicious, delicate flavour that could hold its own next to any lasagne filling. It was one of Holly's favourite meals but it was a lot of trouble to go to just for herself, so she didn't make it often.

The oven was still hot from roasting the aubergine so Holly cracked the door while she separated the eggs. Making meringue was one of Holly's favourite things to do. It was somewhere in-between cooking, science and magic. Beating in enough air and adding things in the right order and at the right speed can turn egg whites and sugar into meringue. It seems impossible until it happens and then suddenly you look down and you have a huge bowl of beautiful, glossy meringue in front of you. Holly spooned this glorious mixture into a jumbo piping bag fitted with a wide star nozzle and started making even, dainty swirls on a large baking sheet. Rather than one per person Holly was opting to do three mini pavlovas for each guest, each with different toppings. This meant that she needed to make about a hundred small meringue nests, to give herself a few spares in case any broke or chipped. Making each swirl of shining meringue even was a very soothing task and Holly didn't notice her arms aching until she stepped back and surveyed her work. Perfect. She slipped the trays into the oven and turned off the heat all together. She wasn't familiar with this oven and would need to watch the meringues quite closely but she decided that she could allow herself a few minutes break.

Making a quick cup of tea, Holly went outside to walk around in the sunshine. It was a beautiful day and it almost seemed a shame to be spending it in the kitchen. Almost. The Youth Centre was surrounded on three sides by areas of grassland of various sizes. There was a football pitch on one side, lumpy and potholed grass behind and then just a small swathe of grass on the other side separating the centre from the rest of the street. Holly walked around the football pitch side to the front, keeping in the sun. The front of the buildings only had parking spaces and the bike rack but its low perimeter wall gave Holly somewhere to sit and drink her tea. There were no bikes or cars here now, except her own van and Joe's SUV. A broken bike lock and a few empty water bottles littered the ground but for the most part Joe kept the centre in good repair and rubbish free. Holly enjoyed looking out over the football pitch and the grass beyond it. Without the squeal of children playing, it was peaceful here. All too soon her mug was empty and the kitchen was calling. She needed to get back to her meringues and make sure that they were alright.

Peering through the oven door Holly was pleased to see that all of her meringues looked like they were on track. They hadn't spread or collapsed or burnt, they were the same size and shape as when she'd put them in and they all looked to be baking nicely. She would need to keep a close eye on them but she could start preparing the fruit at the same time. The pears and apples needed to be cooked and then cooled so she would start with them. The pears were going to be poached so she peeled them and placed them in a pan of water with the sugar and spices. In a couple of hours they would be perfect.

Holly always felt that it would be better to have too much than not enough, so she peeled, cored and diced more than a dozen apples. They went into a pan with a little brown sugar, a pinch of cinnamon and a splash of water to keep them from sticking. She moved them around the pan gently, careful not to mash them when they eventually started to soften. She tried a tiny piece to check the flavour and then set them aside to cool. The meringue would probably need at least another hour in the oven if not more but Holly could work on her pie base now and have it ready. She worked together butter, flour and sugar with her hands until it formed a sandy breadcrumb mixture. It was a long and messy process but Holly had never found that knives or pastry cutters were quite as effective. For a dinner like this she was happy to take the time to get everything perfect. Grabbing a lined pan she carefully pressed in her mixture to the base in an even layer. This too was then set aside. Except for her tea break she had now been cooking for hours and she was tired and hungry. It always worked like that, she would be completely absorbed in her cooking and then suddenly find herself finished or just in a lull of activity and realise that she was famished. Maggie used to joke that Holly could break her leg and so long as she was baking she wouldn't notice a thing.

Knowing that it would be a long day and that she wouldn't be able to nip out, Holly had planned ahead. Stashed in the fridge was a can of diet coke and a salt beef, cheese and pickles sandwich along with a big bag of crisps. Grabbing her food and taking one last quick look at everything to check that it was all progressing as it should, Holly set off back outside to find somewhere to indulge in her own simple meal. Despite being a professional cook, Holly rarely made anything fancy for herself. She tended towards sandwiches and packet noodles, saving the real cooking for her customers. Although she wasn't constantly indulging in fancy treats, Holly was happy with her setup. If she was totally honest, she loved sandwiches and packet noodles. She could bake a perfect croissant, but she was still happy with a few pieces of toast and her mother's home made jam.

Holly tucked into her meal with gusto, her mind wandering casually around the idea of making some jams herself this year. If she made enough maybe some of her customers would stock some in their cafes to sell. It wouldn't hurt to look for additional revenue streams.

"Hello! How's it going?"

Holly jumped and nearly dropped half her sandwich on the floor but she recovered quickly and the sandwich, thankfully, remained intact.

"Oh Joe! Hi!" she greeted him with a relieved smile.

Joe chuckled good-naturedly at her obvious alarm.

"Sorry, I didn't mean to scare you. I just stuck my head in the kitchen to see how you were getting on but you were nowhere to be seen." He saw her look of panic, "I didn't touch anything, don't worry."

Holly relaxed slightly,

"It's all going well, everything is on track. Who's going to be serving the food? It's not buffet style is it?" With advance warning Holly could handle a buffet no problem, but she hadn't used pretty trays for the lasagnes or brought any of her fancy serving dishes.

"No, no! I've enlisted a few of the more coordinated teens to carry the plates and things out. It's good for them to have some responsibility and helps the donors to remember why they do it," he assured her.

"That's a great idea! I remember helping out at things like this when I was younger," she told him.

"Your mum could always be relied on to rope you and your brothers in to whatever was needed."

They both smiled at the shared memories.

"So you don't need help with anything?" he asked.

"No, everything's going great! I should get back in there but it's going perfectly so far," she told him.

She stood up and they walked back towards the building together. Holly looked around and noticed that the rubbish she'd spotted earlier had already been cleared up.

"You really do look after this place well Joe," she commented.

He looked at her for a minute like he was wondering if she was mocking him.

"I do my best. I'll let you get back on with your cooking."

Walking back into the kitchen Holly was met by the subtle smell of cooked meringue. She dashed over to the oven and peering through the door she was pleased to see that they still looked perfect. Opening the door slowly she reached in and retrieved the trays of beautiful white swirls. She put them on the counter on the other side of the kitchen and transferred her attention to the pears. Testing one very carefully with a knife she found that they were softening beautifully but hadn't quite reached their peak. She left them to it and started work on the strawberries. Several large punnets of bright red berries needed to be washed, stemmed and chopped. Holly got to work. It was methodical and repetitive and she kept going until she judged that she had enough and her hands were stained red. The strawberry smell was mixing with the sweet smell of the meringue and the whole kitchen smelt divine. A thought was tugging at the edge of Holly's mind but she couldn't quite see it. Its shape was still hazy and indistinct so she pushed it aside telling it firmly to come back when it was done. The chopped strawberries were drizzled with a little juice from a lemon and sprinkled with sugar, creating the appearance of crystals amid the lush red surface of the fruits. It was beautiful and it would look even more beautiful paired with pure white meringue and fluffy whipped cream. The strawberries went into the fridge to keep cool and Holly checked the pears again. They were perfect. She took them off the heat and put them on a trivet on the windowsill, opening the window a crack so that they could be cooled off faster by the breeze.

Everything was going to schedule but it was coming up on the final crunch time and nerves were bubbling in Holly's stomach. It was always exciting but a certain amount of trepidation was unavoidable. All it would take would be for one timing to be a few minutes out and something could burn or grow cold or worse, be undercooked. Food poisoning was definitely Holly's worst case scenario. It had never happened but Holly held a small pebble of fear in her chest with every catering job.

There was a little over an hour to go before the food would be served. The vegetables to go alongside the lasagne and the summer salads were the last things that needed preparing. Once the spring greens were thoroughly washed Holly sliced them thinly and set them in a large colander to wait. Now the asparagus needed to be washed and trimmed and then that too could be set aside. The summer salads consisted of mixed leaves, ripe plum tomatoes, mozzarella pearls and sliced peaches, all drizzled with a delicious balsamic dressing.

Finally, everything was ready to cook. Holly looked around her at the sumptuous meal waiting to be assembled. The summer salad was mixed and waiting to be distributed onto plates. The lasagnes were standing ready to go into the oven. The side vegetables were placed next to their pots of water. The desserts had most of their component parts ready and just needed to be put together with a few extra bits while people enjoyed their mains.

Holly checked the time and then took a deep breath. She could do this.

The lasagnes slid into the oven and Holly closed the door. Now it was a dance of timings. The salads were easy enough, but the spring greens with lemon and garlic needed to be ready at the same time as the asparagus and lasagne.

This all needed to be plated up and reach the tables still hot but without the greens turning to mush. If she was totally honest with herself Holly adored the tension. She thrived on the bustle and rush. Her usually conciliating manner fell away and she ordered her fleet of teens around with ease. Joe had selected a good group. It was made up of three girls and three boys, all wearing white shirts and black trousers. Most were in black jeans but really it was just to make them look presentable for the donors and to make them feel professional for themselves. One of the girls sauntered up to Holly after the salads had all been distributed. She had short red hair and she watched with interest as Holly added the asparagus to a steamer.

"Joe said you used to help out serving at events like this too," she stated.

"Yep, I was a server when I was your age. I must have worked a dozen of these things," Holly agreed.

The girl nodded at the confirmation.

"Do you like being a cook?" she asked.

"I do. I love it actually. I mostly bake but events like this are always amazing when they come along," Holly told her.

Again the girl nodded as though to herself.

"Did you hear about that drug dealer that got killed?" she asked abruptly.

"What?!" Holly spun round to face the girl but just then Joe appeared, wrangling the kids to go and fetch the now empty salad plates. They were back in no time but the main course needed to be taken straight out to the waiting diners so it wasn't until the lasagne had all been served and Holly had started the dessert prep that she was able to resume the conversation. She beckoned the girl over to where she stood at the hob, slowly stirring dark chocolate sauce.

"What do you know about Terry Wood?" she asked her.

"I don't know anything, everyone knows about the body in the woods."

"You do know something, you called him a drug dealer," Holly countered.

The girl shifted a little uncomfortably and glanced back towards the other servers who were standing in a cluster by the door chatting amongst themselves.

"Well yeah, but everyone knew that."

"Did he sell drugs to anyone you know?" Holly asked curiously.

Now the girl looked absolutely panicked. Holly could tell she was going to lose her so she back-pedalled as quickly as possible.

"Ok, don't worry about that. Do you know of any fights? Any problems with anyone?" she asked instead.

"No. Nothing like that." She looked sincere and relieved to be able to answer without incriminating anyone or getting her friends in trouble.

Holly thought for a moment, still stirring rhythmically.

"Did he sell drugs here at the youth centre?" she asked eventually.

The girl paused but then nodded slightly, her lips tightly pursed. Well that wasn't really surprising, Terry's main customers all through school had been other school kids. It made sense that this was a market he was still targeting. Holly was surprised Joe hadn't put a stop to it however.

"Did Joe know?" The girl's forehead creased for a moment before she answered.

"He can't have can he? He'd have never let him come anywhere near here if he knew."

"No, no I suppose you're right." But maybe someone had objected to Terry supplying the town's children with drugs. Holly certainly objected to it and she could understand if other people had too. But would someone kill Terry for it? That was the question.

Holly turned back to her chocolate sauce, her head spinning with questions. She did her best to push them away for now: she needed to focus. A formal dinner was not the time to solve a murder, she needed to keep her mind on the food. The main course would be finished soon and there would only be a short gap between that and dessert. Once the sauce was finished she moved it to the back of the hob to wait. She set out thirty dessert plates on the central counter and placed three perfect meringues on each. She put a dollop of freshly whipped cream on each one and then started spooning on her toppings. One meringue on each plate got a spoonful of the strawberries, one got the apple mixture and some of the beautiful buttery pie crust she had baked earlier crumbled over it. The last meringue was her favourite combination, a couple of thin slices of the poached pears, some toasted hazelnuts and a generous drizzle of the chocolate sauce. Three separate flavours, each absolutely delicious. Dessert is the last part of the meal, it should be a showstopper.

The teens had loaded the plates from the starters and mains into the industrial dishwasher but Holly had kept an eye out and had been pleased to see that almost every plate had come back clean. It was a wonderful feeling to know that thirty people were happy and well fed right now because of her. Food was its own kind of magic.

Once they'd all been collected Holly helped to load the dessert plates into the washer then sent the teens to check with Joe if there was any clear-up still to do in the main hall. Once they were all occupied gathering stray napkins, putting away tables and chairs and sweeping up, Holly could set about returning the kitchen to order in peace.

She always cleaned and washed up as she went but there was everything from the complex meringue dish still to deal with. She washed the baking trays and the bowls from the strawberries and cream. The pans from the pears, apples and sauce were scrubbed next and then stacks and stacks of clean plates and glasses were put away. Holly carried a couple of bags-full of rubbish out to the big industrial bin at the back of the building and then there were just the final details to go. The surfaces had one last spray and wipe down and then Holly packed up all of her things to take out to the van. It had been a long day and she was exhausted. The adrenalin had faded and her whole body ached. She was just packing away the last of her things when she heard someone walking up behind her. In the dark. In a deserted car park. She spun around with a gasp, brandishing a baking tray in front of her like a shield.

Standing before her was a teenager with short red hair and a look of disdain.

Holly straightened up trying to look as though she hadn't done anything embarrassingly over the top.

"Oh hello again!" Holly attempted.

"Hi."

The look of disdain was unchanged.

"Can I help you with something?" Holly asked.

The girl gave a sigh that indicated that she very much doubted it, but she continued anyway.

"Last year there was this girl. She got in a car accident and died."

"I remember, Debbie something," Holly agreed.

"That's right. Well, she was taking drugs when it happened. My mum's a nurse and she was working the night that girl was brought in to the hospital. Afterwards she sat me down and had this big talk with me about drugs and stuff, about how dangerous it all is," the girl told her.

"Why are you telling me this?" Holly asked.

"You were asking about Terry," the girl explained.

"And you think it's related?"

"Well, it might not be. But when my mum was talking to me she asked if I knew him. I didn't then, I hadn't started playing netball here yet, so she just dropped it and didn't say anything else about him. She just kept talking about that girl's parents, how they were screaming and crying in the hospital." Even now the girl looked shaken at the memory. Holly suspected that as far as 'drugs talks' went, this one had probably been pretty successful.

"Ok... thank you. Thank you for telling me. What's your name?" Holly asked her.

"I'm Lydia. Pearsons."

"I'm Holly Abbot."

Holly smiled at the girl who gave a half smile half shrug in response and then turned to go. Holly waited a moment, watching her walk over and get in a car, just to make sure she was safe. She was still feeling a little jumpy. Keeping her keys in her hand she nipped back inside to say goodbye to Joe before heading home. He was in the main hall setting some sporting activity up for the following day. He was dragging huge equipment bags out of the store cupboard and the teenaged servers all appeared to have left.

"Hi Joe! I was just about to head home but is there anything else you need me to do?" she asked him.

"No no! You've done enough! The food was marvellous! That caterer getting ill was an absolute blessing! Well, for me at least!" He chuckled to himself and came forward to shake Holly's hand.

Looking at her a little more closely he asked, "Is everything alright?"

"Oh it was amazing, I'm just exhausted!" she assured him.

"Well you get off home then and I'll see you soon. Thank you so much for tonight, I'll mail the cheque to you."

"Thanks Joe, really, it was great!"

She turned to go but at the last moment she turned back. "Joe?"

He looked back at her questioningly.

"Can I ask you something?"

He nodded.

"When did you last see Terry?"

He looked relieved, like he'd been expecting her to ask about something else entirely.

"On the Tuesday. He stopped by here about two o'clock and I had a chat with him and then he left."

"What did you talk about?"

"Oh, nothing much. Like you said, we were friends." He looked sad and Holly couldn't bear to push much harder. One more question and then home.

"Did he leave his bike here?"

Terry looked surprised but answered quickly.

"No. He left on it."

"Ok, well, thanks again Joe."

He watched her walk back across the hall and out the door.

Chapter 12

The drive home was blessedly uneventful and in no time
Holly was back in her flat. Exhaustion threatened to
overwhelm her but she was starving hungry too. She decided
to eat something before bed and she'd smuggled home a
portion of leftover lasagne so all she needed to do was heat it
up. She stuck it in the microwave and used the three minutes
that it was slowly rotating to change into some pyjamas and
wash her face. Grabbing a blanket and her bowl of lasagne
she curled up on the sofa in front of the TV and started
tucking in to her much deserved dinner. It was absolutely
delicious and Holly felt a warm rush of pride. Finishing her
food she decided to just watch a little bit more Diagnosis
Murder and then head to bed.

Holly woke at about 2am as her neck and back both
made their complaints known about the vertical sleeping
position. She stumbled off to the bedroom and collapsed into
bed, revelling in the comfort of a good mattress and a duvet.
Within moments she had fallen into a deep sleep, plagued by
parents crying in hospital corridors.

Holly woke next morning feeling foggy and confused. It
took her a moment to work out how to switch off her alarm.

Sunday wasn't a deliveries day so at least she didn't need to leap up and start baking, but her muscles were sore from the previous day's labours and she was reluctant to get out of bed at all. After wrestling with herself for a few minutes Holly settled on a compromise. Dragging herself upright she headed for the kitchen. She put on the kettle, put a couple of slices of bread into the toaster and fetched milk, butter and jam from the fridge. She selected a mug and a plate from the cupboard and soon she had a steaming mug of tea and a plate of toast ready to be consumed. She settled these on her bedside table and went and grabbed her notebook and a pen from her bag.

Going back to bed, she snuggled down under the duvet, leaning back against the wall with her small notebook on her lap. Happily munching her way through her toast she made pages and pages of notes on everything she knew. She had notes on all of the people she had spoken to, what they had told her and what else she knew about them. She made a very rough timeline of Terry's movements on the Tuesday, leaving spaces to hopefully fill in when she was able to find out more. Currently she had him leaving his and Kim's, a brief visit with Joe and then hours and hours unaccounted for before he was found in the woods early the following morning. Next she had a list of the places that she knew he'd worked in the past couple of years, with stars next to the ones he had stolen from. Finally there was a whole double page spread dedicated to the family of the girl who had died in the car accident. So far the pages were blank but that would be the task for today. Holly intended to find out everything she could about Debbie and what had happened to her. She couldn't remember drugs being mentioned in the news article but she couldn't recall it very well. She didn't know the girl who had died and so she'd only paid it a passing interest. It might turn out to be unrelated but Lydia's mother had mentioned Terry by name so Holly decided it was worth the time to look into it further. It wasn't as though she had any other clear avenues of investigation before her.

Finishing her last swig of tea Holly moved to the living room and pulled out her laptop from its home under the coffee table. Switching it on, she gave it a few minutes to carry out the inevitable updates and went to make a second mug of tea. Holly didn't use her laptop often, favouring the convenience of her phone for recipe hunting and general internet browsing, but she felt that real research called for real equipment. Fresh cup of tea in hand she walked back to the sofa and saw that the updates were still going: 33% and counting. There was time for more toast. Eventually Holly was settled on the sofa, a half-consumed plate of toast next to her, untouched tea set beside her laptop and a look of rapt attention on her face.

To be sure of scooping the story early, the article that she remembered seeing had just given the basic tragic facts. Nineteen-year-old Debbie Hall had been involved in a car crash in the early hours of the morning and unfortunately she had not survived. Subsequent articles had elaborated further however. She had been driving her father's car and she had been under the influence of narcotics. Terry Wood wasn't mentioned anywhere but Holly supposed that that made sense. Newspapers couldn't go around printing that individuals were drug dealers, even if they were. Presumably the police hadn't linked Terry to Debbie's death or he would have been mentioned in at least one article, but maybe that didn't mean anything. Holly's town wasn't exactly rife with crime; the local police could well have been trundling along, brimming with ineptitude for years.

The article gave Debbie's parents names as Michael and Susan Hall. It mentioned that Michael worked as owner of H.J. Construction but no profession was listed for Susan. Holly jotted all of this information down in her notebook and continued reading. There were quotes from other people who had known Debbie, lots of 'I just can't believe this happened' and 'that poor family' and 'it's such a loss', but no names were given. Holly moved on to the next article; she wanted to be sure that if there was someone out there who might be looking for revenge for Debbie, she knew about them. The next article she looked at basically just rehashed the information already disclosed, trying to feed public interest. It did mention the 'scourge of drug abuse present amongst the youth of our town' but no names or details. The police were called upon to crack down hard on substance abuse and prevent any further tragic loss of young life, but again any details were vague or just absent.

The next article Holly found was from a different paper and was less dramatic in its content. This writer seemed to be more of a practical nature. There was less of a calling to arms but more facts, and Holly found two pieces of information detailed here very interesting indeed. One was the hospital that Debbie had been taken to after the crash. Holly made a note of this to potentially track down Lydia Pearsons' mother and find out how Terry was connected to everything. The second was that Debbie had worked for a local gym. Unless they were being very loose with their definition of the word 'local', this meant that Debbie had worked for Jack at the leisure centre.

Chapter 13

An hour later Holly found herself walking around the supermarket, staring at the shelves, bordering on despair. She'd already loaded her trolley with medjool dates, chia seeds, flax seeds, raisins and oats. She'd decided that if she was going to have to go back to the leisure centre, then the healthy treat samples that she'd promised Jack would be the perfect cover. She'd felt good about it at the time but now that she was here looking at the food in the shop, she was starting to think that 'healthy treats' was a contradiction in terms. Holly's baking had always focused on how to get the best possible taste, rather than the lowest possible calorie count. This was definitely going to be a challenge but not one that Holly was feeling particularly enthusiastic about. She combed the aisles looking for more healthy ingredients or maybe just some inspiration. Maybe she could try a couple of obviously healthy options and then a couple of healthy versions of traditional treats. She grabbed some nuts and dried fruits, thinking that she could make her own granola for granola bars.

Fruit was healthy! She grabbed a few packs of strawberries and raspberries to experiment with, along with some apples and pears. She would have liked to try something with peaches but they weren't really in season yet. Now, back to the confectionery aisle for some good quality dark chocolate. Along with some coconut oil and some bee pollen that Holly saw in the nuts section and grabbed at the last minute, it was the most unusual shop that Holly had ever done. Usually Holly did research first and started planning a recipe before setting foot in a shop, but in this case Holly suspected that she would be more constrained by which healthy ingredients she could readily get hold of than anything else. It was no good getting her heart set on making some variation of a sprouted wheat cake if she couldn't get any sprouted wheat (whatever that was!).

Holly lugged her purchases home and laid them all out on the kitchen counter tops around her. She slowly surveyed them, waiting for inspiration to hit. Nothing jumped out and eventually she shrugged to herself. Ok, maybe a granola. Making the third mug of tea of the day she sat down to look up dozens of granola recipes and formulate her own based on what she'd bought and anything else she could scrounge up from her existing food stores. Finally she settled on a simple granola recipe to try, then she could taste it and adjust accordingly. Once she had a tray of the oaty, nutty concoction before her, she scooped up a spoonful and gave it a go. It was too sweet, the individual flavours of the ingredients was being obscured by the honey, and more honey would be used to form it into bars. Holly started again, this time using less honey and a pinch more salt, along with some lemon zest. This batch turned out better. Much more experimenting and adjusting would be needed before Holly was happy with them but Holly wanted to have something to show Jack soon, so she decided to keep them as they were for now and move on to a new creation.

Next she made some healthy peanut butter cups. She had made something similar once before so she had a head start on the recipe finagling and these turned out well. The base was blitzed peanut butter, dates, ground almonds and oats and the top layer was dark chocolate, melted, mixed with a little coconut oil and poured over the top of the base and put in the fridge to set. They were delicious, reasonably healthy and so rich that you only wanted one anyway. It was a good combination.

There was still a large array of ingredients spread out around the kitchen but Holly had no idea what to do with them. Running her fingers through her hair in frustration she decided that it might be time to call in reinforcements. After a brief phone call Kat was on her way round, 'taste buds at the ready' as she put it. Over the years Kat had acted as taster for what felt like hundreds of recipes. She tended to like most things, but Holly felt that the moral support was invaluable. What would she do when Kat was gone? Pushing the thought aside Holly mixed some of the second batch of granola with a little honey, pressed it into a tin and sprinkled it with some of the bee pollen. When Kat arrived she had a few granola bars and some peanut butter cups for her to sample.

"Ooh! Treats! Wait, what are these? They do not look like cakes." Kat was turning her nose up at the bars, holding one up in front of her as though it were something slimy that she didn't want to get too close to.

"It's a granola bar Kat. Jack wants some healthier options to offer at the leisure centre cafe. He's hoping to entice the gym-goers to stop for food too."

Kat looked outraged, "I feel lied to! Betrayed! You lured me round here with the promise of cake and cookies and now it's *granola*?!" She said it like it was the most disgusting thing in the world and Holly couldn't help but smile.

"I never said anything about cake or cookies. I just said I was trying out new recipes."

Kat narrowed her eyes but remained pointedly silent as though this question of semantics was beneath her. Holly sighed, "At least try one."

Kat reluctantly brought the bar up to her mouth and took a dainty bite, followed by a huge mouthful. Chewing happily she managed a muffled, "Oh! It's pretty good!" before going back in for another bite. Kat set about making them each a cup of tea while Holly talked her through the healthy ingredients and tried to figure out other things that she could make with them. They tried to think of healthy options they'd seen online or in other cafes but really they'd both ignored them in favour of buttery, chocolatey goodness. Once the teas were ready they both pulled out their phones, googled variations of 'healthy treats,' and scrolled through the results looking for inspiration.

"Maybe some kind of a muffin," Kat eventually offered.

"Yeah, that might be good. I already do muffins so it

wouldn't be too much extra work. I could use banana as a natural sweetener..."

Holly was already rising as she spoke, making her way over to her fruit to see what she could use. She had a punnet of blueberries and she was pleased to see that she even had some bananas that were getting brown spots. It would have been better if the peels had turned almost fully brown but she could experiment with what she had for now. She contemplated using some raspberries too but decided that without sugaring them the raspberries would be too tart when cooked. She used a whole-wheat flour and made some oat flour to go with it too. When she had a batter made up she gave it a quick taste and decided to add a little coconut sugar. It was a sweetener, but at least it was a healthier option and she didn't want to completely sacrifice taste in favour of small waistlines.

She stirred through the blueberries, ladled portions into muffin cases and slid them into the oven with a sprinkling of oats on top.

"So, how's the investigation going?" Kat asked, finishing the last of her tea and setting the mug down in front of her.

"I'm still talking to people. It seems like almost everyone who knew Terry hated him. There certainly isn't a shortage of people who might be happy to see him bumped off, but I can't imagine any of them actually doing it."

"Can you imagine anyone killing someone?" Kat asked. It was a good point. Holly had never experienced real violence outside of TV dramas and the notion of someone actually doing harm to another human being felt utterly foreign somehow. Had anything that she'd found out about Terry so far been enough to get him killed? Terry had stolen from Rebecca and Gladys and he'd stolen from customers at the garage. He'd been selling drugs to kids at the youth centre and it was possible that he'd sold Debbie the drugs that had caused her crash. For all Holly knew he'd been selling drugs to other people too, maybe people who were dangerous enough to hit him in the head with a rock and leave him in the woods.

Holly very briefly ran through everything that she'd learned for Kat's benefit. When she'd finished speaking Kat had a look on her face that was hard to identify.

"What?" Holly asked.

"I don't know. I guess... I knew that you were looking into this but I suppose that I just didn't realise you'd be so good at it."

Holly felt a gentle warming of pride. It turned out that it could be quite nice to surprise people.

"I don't exactly feel like I'm about to crack it though. It's like the more I learn the more I realise how big people's lives are. There's just more and more to find out."

"What's the next thing that you need to find out then?" Kat asked pragmatically.

"Debbie Hall. Terry did a lot of bad things and upset a lot of people, but it's all quite small stuff in the scheme of things. Debbie Hall is different; she died. If Terry was involved, then that's a real reason that he might have been killed."

"So you think that it might have been somebody who knew Debbie? Someone who blamed him for her death?" Kat looked saddened by the prospect and Holly knew just how she felt.

"I know. If that's why Terry was murdered I think I'd understand it. I'm not sure that I would want someone who loved her to be arrested. She was nineteen years old, she had parents, she had her whole life ahead of her. That sounds corny doesn't it, you hear it all the time but it's true. Nineteen is so young, life is just starting and then it was all just gone in an instant."

They were saved from their descent into melancholy by the oven timer going. Holly rushed over and checked the muffins. They were perfectly golden and springy. Taking them out of the oven she transferred them to a cooling rack.

"These will need a few minutes to cool before we can try them."

"Time for more tea!" Kat leapt up and went to the kettle. They didn't resume their conversation until they each had a steaming mug of tea and a warm muffin in front of them. Kat eyed her muffin suspiciously before taking a bite.

"Are you sure this is healthy? It just seems like a normal muffin to me."

"Good! That's the idea! It needs work but it's a good start," Holly responded.

"So if this is all about Debbie, who could it have been? Her parents?" Kat asked.

"Yes, but not just them. Obviously they would have a motive but I found out something interesting in one of the news articles about the crash. Someone I've already spoken to had a connection to Debbie Hall." Holly left it there, taking another bite of muffin and enjoying drawing out the suspense.

"Who?!" Kat had never been a particularly patient person.

"Jack," Finally Holly answered.

"At the leisure centre?"

Holly nodded, "Yes, Debbie worked there. The leisure centre could even be how she and Terry met. I'll need to check if they were both working there at the same time."

Holly went to her notebook and checked back through all of her notes.

"No, it looks like Terry worked there after Debbie had already died. But it still means that Jack has a connection with both Debbie and Terry. He was really strange about Terry when I asked about him, he couldn't get away from me fast enough."

"Strange how? What did he say?" Kat asked.

Holly thought for a moment, "He seemed angry. For a moment there, when he thought I might be friends with Terry, I think he was considering firing me. Then he basically told me not to have anything to do with him."

Kat looked shocked, "Wow! That's a pretty extreme reaction!"

"I know, and then he just took off. A waitress heard us talking and she basically said that it was about drugs. She made it sound like a moral thing, like Jack doesn't like drugs because they're bad for you and he's all about health. Maybe it's more than that though, maybe Jack hated Terry because he held him responsible for the death of someone he knew."

"Do you think they were involved?" Kat asked.

"Who?"

"Jack and Debbie. It would explain Jack being willing to kill over it. You don't commit murder for a standard employee do you?" Kat had a good point. Jack was only mid-twenties, Debbie would have been twenty by now if she'd lived, it wouldn't be impossible. Again Holly found herself questioning whether she really wanted the guilty person caught, but there was one thing Dan had always been right about: the law is the law for a reason. It was just hard realising that even good people aren't all good and bad people aren't all bad. Shades of grey.

"Maybe they were involved, maybe they weren't. Maybe Jack has nothing to do with this or maybe he does. Either way I need more information," Holly finally stated. Confusing as the situation was morally, the plan was straightforward.

"So are you going to go back and talk to Jack again?" asked Kat.

Holly held up a muffin, "That's the plan."

Holly now had blueberry banana muffins, peanut butter cups and granola bars. She wanted one more treat to add to the mix and she settled on a healthier variation of one of her existing favourites, strawberry crumble slices. She used grass-fed butter for the base because the internet sincerely assured her that this was healthier than the usual stuff and worth the exorbitant price tag. She added oats to fill out the base and crumble topping mixture, and limit the white flour and butter per slice. The strawberry filling would usually consist of chopped strawberries, stewed over a low heat with plenty of sugar but instead Holly used fresh fruit. This would hopefully allow the strawberries to keep more of their natural sweetness and taste good, even without any added sugar. Again they went into the oven and Holly and Kat sat down to wait. They had exhausted the murder talk already and Holly was more than ready to think about something else for a little while.

"How's Dan?" Holly asked, surreptitiously watching her friend whilst nervously waiting for an answer. She knew that she was presenting a possible opening for Kat to tell her that she was leaving but instead her friend just shrugged.

"He's fine." Then Kat's eyes narrowed slightly and Holly detected suspicion in her gaze. "Why? Has he said something?"

"I haven't spoken to him since Dad got released by the police," Holly reassured her, "I was just wondering how you two are doing."

"Better than ever," Kat smiled. "I knew! I always knew that Dan and I were meant to be. He was just so gorgeous and so serious all the time, how could we not be?" She threw up her hands in a carefree gesture, and smiled in such a way that Holly felt almost as though she were intruding on something personal by witnessing it. It still felt strange to Holly but she had to admit that Kat and Dan were actually a wonderful couple. They brought out the best in each other and made each other sincerely happy. Maybe if she saw them together more often she would get used to the idea. Holly mused on this while sipping the last of her almost cold tea. Kat broke into her thoughts in her usual battering ram style, clicking her fingers next to Holly's face.

"Hey! Holly! A one to one conversation is not the time for day dreaming!"

"Sorry, I was just thinking about relationships," Holly admitted.

"Good! When are you going to try one?" Kat looked at her intently, waiting for an answer.

Holly sighed, "I just don't meet people. I'm busy. And even if I did meet someone I wouldn't know what to say or what to do or... anything." With that Holly flopped down onto her arms on the counter in front of her, as though even the act of *talking* about a social interaction was utterly exhausting to her.

Kat laughed and propped her friend back up in her seat.

"When you meet someone you like you'll figure all the rest out. But the point is you need to actually try meeting someone. It's never going to happen if you never try. When's the last time you even made a new friend."

Holly looked a little indignant now, "I make friends! I made a new friend recently in fact." Looking very smug now, Holly took a nonchalant swig of tea, but the effect was somewhat spoiled by the involuntary grimace at finding it cold. She got up and went over to the kettle to start their third mugs of the brew, leaving an irate Kat behind her.

"Who?! You made a friend and you didn't tell me?!

Who who who?!" As Kat's voice became increasingly shrill, Holly smiled more broadly.

"Well, they're funny, kind, a good cook, an excellent gardener, very caring and witty... and about eighty years old. Her name is Rebecca."

A look of comprehension dawned and Kat laughed, "One of the women that Terry worked for!"

Holly chuckled in response, "Yes, when I went to see her she acted like she had no idea who I was and she was absolutely terrifying. She made me think of a witch in a fairytale but actually it was all just an act."

"An act? You're sure she's not just senile?"

Holly shook her head, "No, far from it. It was like a game; she was playing a part for fun but actually she was amazing and I stayed for ages just talking to her. She had this incredible life with her husband. They had kids and grand-kids and great-grand-kids and she has pictures all over her house of her family and artwork from the children and it was just beautiful. And the garden! Kat, I've never seen anything like it! It was incredible! She and her husband did it all themselves and it took years but it's worth it, it's amazing to see! It would be wonderful to have a marriage like that."

Kat smiled on as she enthused about Rebecca and her garden but as she finished on her somewhat wistful note, Kat sighed in exasperation.

"That's exactly what I'm talking about Holly! It would be one thing if you didn't want a relationship, but you do! You don't find great love by sitting at home baking."

"Well then how do you find great love?" she countered,

"In pubs or bars? Maybe clubbing? Or you could fix me up. Do you have someone stellar in mind for me to spend my life with?"

Kat looked chagrined, "No, but you have to get out there. Talk to people. The more people you know, the more chance of meeting the right one. Your world could be bigger than it is Holly."

Holly knew that her friend was right but that didn't make taking her advice any easier. Finally, she spoke again.

"Could we go shopping soon? For clothes I mean."

Kat gaped at her in silence. For a long time she didn't say anything at all, like Holly's request was some kind of shy woodland creature that might be startled and flee if she wasn't careful. Eventually she nodded gently and very quietly said, "Sure, ok."

Then they both just sat quietly with their teas, waiting for the strawberry slices to finish baking.

Chapter 14

When Holly had a platter assembled of her new healthy baked goods, she gave it one last critical look and put the cover on. She would usually spend at least a week working on a single recipe, trying it out and adjusting it and forcing samples on her parents and of course on Kat. This time, she needed to be quick so that she could use it as an excuse to go back and talk to Jack again. The perfectionist in her was finding it very difficult to present a customer with food that was anything less than flawless, but she consoled herself that she would be very clear that these treats were a work in progress. Holly hadn't attempted healthy baked goods before and it was entirely believable that she might want a little extra guidance.

She was feeling a lot more comfortable than last time she'd rolled up to the leisure centre. This time she had an actual plan and a tray full of reasons to be there. Approaching the reception desk, Holly hovered in what she hoped was a carefree and nonchalant manner but suspected came across as cripplingly awkward lurking. Once the receptionist had finished with the women in front who were headed to a water aerobics class, Holly stepped forward and asked to see Jack.

"Do you have an appointment with him?"

"No, but I'm one of the suppliers for the cafe and I have some samples he asked to try," she explained.

"Ok, no problem, just wait a moment for me."

The receptionist gave Jack a quick call and then directed Holly to his office. Just like that, she was through. Jack's office was a small room that had the air of being little used. Everything on the shelves was orderly but a little dusty. The desk looked used but there was nothing personal, no pictures or knick-knacks. Jack ushered her in and Holly sat down. Rather than sitting in his chair Jack perched on the edge of the desk. Holly had to admit that the office swivel chair didn't seem right somehow, Jack looked more at home standing or walking. Even perched on the desk he looked as though he may leap up at any moment and start doing star jumps or push-ups or something equally exhausting.

"So! I hear you already have some samples for me! I didn't think you'd be this quick!"

"Well they're not perfect, still a work in progress, but I was hoping you'd check them out and see if I'm on the right track. It's a bit outside of my usual wheel house," Holly admitted.

"Absolutely! What have we got?" Jack asked eagerly.

Holly took the cover off of the tray and pointed to each offering in turn.

"There's granola squares, peanut butter cups, blueberry and banana muffins and strawberry slices. I brought some slices with glaze and some without. The glaze isn't healthy but it does really tip the taste over the top."

"These all look amazing! Are you sure they're healthy?" Jack chuckled.

"Well I guess it depends on your definition. None of them is a kale smoothie, let's say that." Jack laughed again and Holly felt relieved that it was all going well so far. Obviously she wanted her cooking to be well received but there was also the matter of questions that needed answering and it would be much easier if Jack were in a good mood.

"I've got a list of the ingredients for each. I wasn't sure if you had any allergies or anything, and I thought you could check if there's anything in them that you're not happy with," she told him.

Jack scanned through the list of ingredients looking impressed. "You've got some good things in here and it looks like there's not too much sugar. Grass-fed butter too! That's good!"

Holly nodded sagely, silently thanking Google for advising her well.

"Ok," Jack rubbed his hands together, "Which do you advise I start with?"

Holly recommended the granola bar first and Jack took a large bite. As he chewed appreciatively Holly couldn't help but mention a few adjustments that she would make to make them even better.

"This is delicious! And not too sweet either. A lot of granola bars you can buy seem to be all sugar but this is just right, you can really taste the nuts."

Holly glowed with pride. Next Jack sampled one of the

muffins. He was absolutely thrilled with these. Holly's muffins were one of the cafe's best sellers and Jack was delighted to be able to offer a healthy version. Holly couldn't tell if he was more excited to lure health nuts into the cafe or to trick the usual cafe goers into eating healthier food. Either way, he was pleased. The strawberry slice was up next and Jack tried it both with and without the glaze. He agreed that the glazed version tasted better but he was clearly reluctant to add sugar if it could be helped.

"If you know all the amounts of all the ingredients, do you think you could work out the calorie count per slice? If the glaze makes a big difference then we'll leave it off but if the calorie count overall is still low then maybe we could list the calories of the healthy stuff along with the prices. I think that could persuade some of the gym goers!"

It wasn't something Holly had done before, but if it would clinch the extra business then she was happy to give it a try and she could think of at least a few cafes who might be interested in healthier options too. This could be a good move.

"Sure thing, I can at least give it a go!"

Jack was thrilled and was practically bouncing up and down with excitement at the thought of this new facet of the plan when Holly reminded him that there was one thing left to try.

"Jack, you still need to give the peanut butter cups a go."

He looked at them suspiciously. "They look like regular peanut butter cups. I know that peanut butter isn't strictly bad for you, but I know that peanut butter cups are."

Holly laughed and directed his attention back to the ingredients list, "There's no sweetener used, just the dates. There's peanut butter but also ground almonds and oats and a little coconut oil for the consistency. Even the chocolate on top is dark chocolate, 70% cocoa and again with a little coconut oil to make it softer and add some extra creaminess."

Jack was looking her like it was all too good to be true but he took one anyway and took a bite. The look on his face could only be described as pure bliss. He finished the rest of the treat reverently and then gave a happy sigh.

"Peanut butter cups were always my favourite but I haven't had one in years. I started seeing a personal trainer when I was seventeen and he gave me a pretty strict diet to follow. I've relaxed it a bit since then but once you look at the ingredients listed on the pack it's definitely less fun to indulge. But these are incredible! They're so good I can't believe it!"

Holly smiled at his reaction; it was wonderful to see people enjoy food. Maybe healthy cooking wasn't such a bad idea.

"They need to be kept in the fridge but they'll last a couple of weeks. I can do big batches and have them on hand ready so they'd be a great one from my perspective," she told him.

"Oh they are definitely a yes from me. You are a genius in the kitchen Holly." He told her with a smile.

"Thank you," Holly beamed.

"In fact these are all brilliant, I'd love to add each of them to the regular menu as soon as possible. I know you want to make some more changes to them and there's the calorie calculation to do, but when do you think you can have them ready?" he asked.

Holly thought about it for a moment, running through her plans for the coming week in her head,

"I can probably have them ready in a week. That should give me time to adjust the recipes a little and have my testers sample them," she told him.

Jack looked at her questioningly and she laughed.

"Just my parents and my best friend, they've been my official taste testers for years," she explained.

"That's nice! It's so important to have people around you to lend support, and I'm sure they don't mind helping out with cake sampling!" he commented.

"They definitely don't seem to mind helping out with recipe development," Holly agreed, "And it is nice having friends and family so close. What about your family, are they close by?"

"No, it was always just me and my mum growing up and she remarried and moved down south when I was eighteen."

"You didn't want to go with her?" Holly was worried she might be prying but Jack seemed happy to chat and Holly was happy enough to make the most of it.

"No, I started working here part time when I was sixteen and by the time I was eighteen I was offered a full time job. If I'd moved away then and tried to find a job at a gym somewhere else I wouldn't have had the seniority I'd earned here. Here people knew me and trusted me. I found a small flat share with a couple of friends and worked hard, working my way up. I took over managing the place five years later when I was just twenty-three."

"That's amazing! You must miss your mum but you obviously love your job here and this is your home after all. I could never imagine leaving."

"I talk to my mum a few times a week and I see her as often as I can, but she loves where she lives now with her new husband and I love it here. We're all happy and I have a work family," he told her.

"That's great," Holly said, "I suppose it's one of the things that I miss out on working alone, but I have to admit, I've never really seen the appeal of working with other people. Is it nice being in charge of a team?" she asked.

"Being *part* of a team," Jack corrected. "I'm the manager but that's just another role in the team. It's great being a part of a group like this. Everyone who works here is brilliant and I trust them all."

"Debbie Hall used to work here didn't she? I'm sorry to mention it, I just remember the newspapers saying she worked at a local gym. Was it this one?"

Jack sighed, "Yes, she worked here. She was great, an amazing girl. I think about it every day."

"It's so sad. The news articles mentioned drugs; it's such a shame, it seems like such a waste, and she was so young too," Holly trailed off, gently shaking her head.

A look of anger and frustration passed over Jack's face,

"I couldn't believe it when I found out. I know a lot of teenagers think of drugs as no big deal. I guess I bypassed all of that working here, but I was surprised to find out Debbie was involved with drugs at all. I was more surprised that she would drive while taking drugs."

"Is that why you were angry when I mentioned Terry last time I was here?" Holly asked.

"I didn't mean to sound angry, but I guess I was. I take it you know he was a drug dealer then? I had no idea when I gave him the job here and I was livid when I found out! The police were here the other day asking about it. You know that he passed away I take it?"

"Yes," Holly confirmed, "My dad was actually the one who found his body when he was walking the dog."

"Ah! When I was told he'd been killed I wondered why you'd been asking about him but I guess it only makes sense that he would be on your mind."

Holly agreed, pleased that Jack hadn't assumed that she'd suspected him of being involved. "Yes, after my dad found the body he had to spend hours at the police station answering questions. Since then we haven't heard anything, I don't know what the police are doing, but you said they'd been here?" Holly asked. It certainly wouldn't hurt to find out what avenue the police's investigation was going down.

"Yeah, they were here. They wanted to know if I'd ever seen him selling drugs to anyone in particular or if anyone had come here looking for him recently. I wasn't able to help unfortunately. He hasn't worked here in a while now and I didn't know of anyone coming around asking for him even then. I only found out about the drugs because one of the gym goers mentioned it to me quietly after they overheard him offering to sell something to another customer. I didn't ask for names, I just fired him. That might sound harsh but after everything with Debbie I don't think it was. I'm not having anything like that around here."

"I don't think it sounds harsh." They were both quiet for a moment. Holly was thinking about Debbie Hall and she suspected that Jack was doing the same.

"The police didn't ask about anything else? They didn't ask about Debbie?" Holly asked.

Now Jack looked confused, "No, they didn't ask anything more. Why would they ask about Debbie? Terry didn't start working here until after Debbie had already passed away, they never worked together." His brow was furrowed and his eyes were dark, calculating the possibility of a connection between a girl who lost her life to narcotics and a drug dealer in the same town. Something in his expression frightened Holly and on impulse she stepped in to distract him.

"Oh well, it was just a random thought! I'm really glad that you like all of the baked goods!"

Jacks brow cleared a little, though not entirely and the smile that he gave Holly was still troubled but he allowed her to steer the subject back to safer topics.

"Yes, they're all delicious. Thank you again for getting to it so quickly, I'm really pleased," he said.

"No problem!" Holly assured him. "I'll have everything finalised for you as soon as possible and then they'll be ready to be launched in the cafe." Holly noted with wry amusement that she had taken over Jack's usual role in the conversation, leading the way with bouncing exuberance. Rather than challenging this shift, Jack appeared grateful to relinquish the reins for once, as though his mind was still running on other things. Holly said a hasty goodbye and showed herself out. She left Jack still perched on the edge of his desk, as though about to leap up but with nowhere to go.

Chapter 15

Back in her van Holly sat, breathing heavily. Her
conversation with Jack had proved to be very intense. Of all
the people she had spoken to about Terry, no one had
demonstrated the grief that Jack clearly felt for Debbie. Her
death had left a hole in the world that still smarted and
ached. Holly could imagine someone wanting justice for that
pain but it didn't seem to have previously occurred to Jack
that Terry could be connected with Debbie's death. Unless he
was a truly phenomenal actor, or Holly much more gullible
than she had ever supposed, the idea that Holly had planted
was a new one. Holly couldn't quite cross Jack off the
suspect list in case she was wrong but she felt now, that it
was unlikely that he was involved. That left her with
Debbie's parents.

Before Holly was going to go accosting the parents of a
girl who had died, she was going to need a lot more
information. For all she knew, Terry hadn't had anything to
do with Debbie's death. Maybe they hadn't even known one
another. The initial step would need to be tracking down
Lydia's mother, the nurse, and finding out everything she

knew about the night Debbie Hall's car had crashed.

But first things first, Holly's phone was ringing.

"Hello darling" Her mother's voice pulled Holly out of her thoughts.

"Hey mum, what's up?" Holly asked.

"I have something here for you. Rebecca gave it to me at church and asked me to pass it along to you."

"Really? What is it?"

"I don't know darling, it appears to be a tin of biscuits but it may be in disguise."

Rather than riddling that one out, Holly agreed to come over and collect whatever it was from her mother directly.

Arriving at her parents' house Holly was indeed presented with a biscuit tin, but rather than the Scottish Shortbread that the tin promised, it in fact contained the most beautiful lemon bars that Holly had ever seen.

Maggie stared into the tin in wonder.

"Did she make those for you?" she asked in hushed tones.

Holly looked up at her mother, smiling.

"I think she did. They look beautiful, don't they?"

"I can't believe it!" Maggie breathed, "The woman's a menace! She absolutely terrifies me! Every time I speak to her I feel like I'm twelve years old and I've spilt ink on the best rug! How on earth have you got her baking you lemon bars?!" she demanded.

Clearly Rebecca didn't only play the fearsome old lady when people called at her house, Holly thought with a smile.

"Well I made her those biscuits, and I did give her the

lemons," Holly offered by way of an explanation.

It wasn't enough for her mother.

"You gave her lemons?! Why?"

"Well we were talking about them when I went round there and,-"

Maggie cut her off, "You were chatting about lemons?! Are we talking about the same Rebecca?! The Wicked Witch of the Weiss?!"

Holly let out a burst of laughter. "Who?! Who calls her that?!"

"Everyone does!" her mother assured her sincerely, "We all go in fear of her at church!"

Holly enjoyed her mother's theatricality and she carried the lemon bars through to the kitchen chuckling appreciatively.

"Shall we have one with some tea?" Holly offered, already putting the kettle on.

"But you still haven't told me how you tamed the beast!" Maggie cried.

Choosing to ignore her mother, Holly continued making the tea, happily humming to herself. It wasn't until she was presented with a full mug and a lemon bar on a china plate that Maggie condescended to cease her questioning and follow her daughter out into the garden to sit down and enjoy their treats.

"What have you eaten today?" Maggie asked as they sat down. "It's Sunday so I hope you had a proper lunch.

Holly looked at her mother guiltily. "I had a granola bar, a banana muffin, two peanut butter cups and a strawberry slice. Plus about a gallon of tea". Under her mother's critical gaze Holly added a feeble, "They were healthy versions..." and then trailed into shameful silence.

"You are always welcome for Sunday lunch here Holly! Particularly if the alternative is a meal of baked snacks!"

"I know Mum but I was doing a bit of recipe development and I needed to try out some things. It didn't leave a lot of time for lunch and to be honest, after I'd tried everything I'd made I wasn't feeling particularly hungry," Holly explained.

"Recipe development? For anything in particular?"

"Yes, I was talking to Jack the other day and he asked about expanding the range at the leisure centre cafe to include some healthy options."

"Healthy?! Gosh, that's a bit outside of your comfort zone," Maggie exclaimed.

"That's OK though. It was good to experiment a bit and I'm happy with the low calorie recipes so far. They still need a bit of work though."

Maggie gave her daughter a shrewd look but only said, "Well I hope you'll bring me some to try."

"Of course I will. Jack's hoping to launch them in about a week, so I'll bring some round in the next few days to get feedback from you and Dad."

"Lovely darling, and I'm glad to hear you're still drumming up more business. But for now there are much more important things to be thinking about."

Holly looked at her mother questioningly.

"The lemon bars of course!"

Holly chuckled and they both lifted their golden yellow bars to their mouths and took a bite. It was sublime. The lemon flavour was incredible and they were just sweet enough without being cloying. The pastry base was perfect and buttery tasting and the textures throughout were just right.

Maggie stared down at the bar in her hand with a look of wonder.

"Who would have thought that Rebecca Weiss could make something so sweet? Maybe she isn't all bad after all."

Holly sighed in half-feigned exasperation but she too was somewhat in awe of the lemon bars. There was something special about them, some ingredient that she couldn't put her finger on. Making a mental note to ask Rebecca for the recipe, Holly took a sip of tea and settled herself more comfortably in her chair to enjoy the rest of her treat.

There was no chance at all of Maggie allowing her daughter to eat nothing but sweets all day so Holly found herself being persuaded to stay and have dinner at her parents' house. She needed very little persuading of course, but it was nice to be talked into it all the same. On Sundays her mother had always cooked a big roast dinner for lunch and then in the evening the meal would consist of tea, cake and maybe some bread and cheese if anyone felt so inclined. Considering all Holly had had so far that day was cake anyway, Maggie declared that Holly had had enough sweet food and she would put together a plate of leftovers for her. Maggie hadn't really scaled down the roast dinners much since she had all four children at home so there were plenty of leftovers available. Holly and her parents sat around the dining table together, them consuming fruit cake and cups of tea and Holly working her way through a huge plate of roast lamb, potatoes, carrots, cabbage, broccoli and gravy. No one else's roast dinners would ever taste as good to Holly as her mum's.

Sunday tea in the Abbot house was an early meal and it was just coming up to six o'clock when Holly got back to her flat. She gave Rebecca a call, thanked her for the lemon bars and asked for the recipe. Rebecca refused but Holly was confident that with time she would win out. The bars were delicious and would be more than worth the effort. Perhaps a recipe trade could be negotiated, if Holly could find something that Rebecca coveted just as much.

The following morning would be the usual early start with cakes to complete and orders to deliver. Holly had the normal evening preparations to do but compared to her increased workload of the preceding week it felt like a holiday. Putting the TV on and turning it to face towards the kitchen, Holly did her prep in a cheerful haze of Bones re-runs. She was still full of delicious roast, she'd enjoyed the afternoon's visit with her parents and she was feeling elated from the success of her meeting with Jack. On the following day she would complete her deliveries and then go to the hospital and try to track down Lydia's mother and talk to her about Debbie Hall. She was happy, well fed and she had a plan. For the first time in what felt like weeks Holly fell into

Elinor Battersby

a peaceful dreamless sleep.

Chapter 16

Roused by her alarm, Holly sat up in bed and looked around her. She really should do something to decorate her flat soon. Maybe she could paint or get new curtains. Again Holly found the time to condition her hair in the shower but again she'd forgotten her towel in the airing cupboard. As she made the cold, naked dash back to her bedroom, Holly reflected that days were made up of highs and lows. She had to quickly pull on some joggers and a jumper to combat her chilly dampness but her hair did smell amazing. Heading out into the kitchen with woolly-sock-clad feet, Holly set about her morning preparations. On the spur of the moment Holly bagged up a couple of spare sandwiches and some of the raspberry crumb muffins. Along with a couple of cans of diet coke she put them into her bag as a bribe for Lydia's mother to talk to her. In Holly's experience food was the best incentive there was.

The deliveries all went well, no problems or hitches of any kind. Holly chatted with her customers again, she was finding that for the most part they were all lovely people and very easy to get on with. Despite her own expectations Holly found it quite easy to fall into the casual pattern of 'chit-chat' that she had always held back from. She suspected that all of her new-found social skills might be needed to get information from Lydia Pearsons' mother, a practical stranger. Holly had never met Mrs Pearsons and had only met her daughter once. It was a tenuous connection and Holly suspected that to a busy nurse it might count for nothing at all. Add to that the fact that Holly would be asking her to discuss some emotional and private information regarding a bereaved family, and Holly wouldn't be at all surprised if she was completely stonewalled.

Although it might be hopeless, Holly wasn't prepared to let the idea go. Debbie Hall's family and friends could be the best possible suspects in Terry's death, but only if Terry had actually been involved in some way. From what Jack had said, it seemed that the police were focusing pretty exclusively on finding anyone that Terry had been dealing drugs to. Holly didn't think that there was anything that she could do in that respect that the police wouldn't already be doing, but Debbie Hall was a line of investigation that she could follow. If the police hadn't mentioned Debbie, when talking to Jack, at her old place of work then it was possible that they hadn't considered her at all. If Holly didn't look into it then it was possible that no one would.

The hospital was a huge, sprawling building and was about as easy to navigate as the Minotaur's labyrinth. Holly was looking for A&E or Intensive Care, as she was guessing that these were the departments Debbie would have been brought to after the crash. The signs directed her to follow an orange line on the floor, but said line had no qualms at all about abandoning her two minutes into her search. Holly found a new line to follow which also cast her adrift and she was just wishing that she had a ball of string to guide her out when she found a nurses' station that looked relatively calm.

A middle aged woman in floral scrubs was sat at a computer. Holly approached, smiling uncertainly,

"Hello, I wonder if you could help me."

"Lost?" the woman smiled up at her understandingly, "where are you trying to get to? Do you have a referral slip with you?"

"Oh I'm not a patient!" Holly hastened to explain. "I'm looking for someone."

"Come to pick up a patient? Do you know what department they're being treated by?"

Well this wasn't as easy as Holly had hoped.

"No, I'm looking for someone who works here. She's a nurse. Mrs Pearsons. I'm not sure which department she's in and I was just hoping you could point me in the right direction," Holly asked hopefully.

The woman now stared at her in stony silence. Holly realised that she was going to have to give a better explanation.

"I know her daughter and I'm just hoping to have a word with her. With Mrs Pearsons that is, not with her daughter." Holly hurried to explain.

"Her daughter?! Which one? Are they OK?" Now Holly was being looked at with concern bordering on alarm.

"They're fine! It's Lydia that I know. There's not a problem, I just want a word." Holly assured her.

The use of Lydia's name had clearly garnered some trust. The woman now typed something into her computer and checked the result.

"She's supposed to be going on lunch in fifteen minutes. She'll be headed to the cafeteria around then most likely," the nurse informed her.

"Thank you so much!" Holly looked around her, checked the visible signs and turned back to the desk. "Um..."

"Green line," the woman pointed without looking up.

Holly set off in the direction indicated and kept an eye on the floor looking for any sign of green. Towards the end of the corridor a green line appeared from nowhere and Holly set her feet on it and kept walking. Around corners, in and out of lifts, Holly followed the green line until finally it led her to a large room laid out with tables and chairs. Despite the furniture and the serving station along the back wall, the place echoed like a sports gym and this phenomenon served to stifle conversation. People ate in silence with grim expressions on their faces and Holly thought that she had never seen a more depressing eating place in her life. Checking the time Holly saw that she still had about five minutes until Mrs Pearsons' lunch break and so she sauntered over to the food counter to see what was on offer. There was a choice of hot or cold food, the cold consisting of wilted sandwiches in polystyrene boxes and the hot being some kind of mystery meat slurry. None of it was appetising and for the first time Holly dared to hope that her errand may be successful, if this was the alternative to her sandwich and muffin bribe.

Holly loitered, wandering around the edges of the room, one eye on the time and the other on the door. By five past the only new arrivals were three men and two elderly ladies and she was starting to worry that her quarry might not be coming. By ten past she was considering setting out on her search again when a woman walked in who had the same red hair as Lydia Pearsons. She stopped just inside the doorway and Holly saw her give a resigned sigh. Approaching her cautiously Holly saw that she actually looked startlingly like Lydia.

"Excuse me, are you Mrs Pearsons? Lydia's mother?" she asked tentatively.

The woman turned to her in surprise, "Yes, I am. Who are you? Is Lydia OK?"

"Oh, yes! Sorry! It's nothing like that, just, you look so much like her so I recognised you..."Holly trailed off awkwardly before rallying for a second attempt.

"I was hoping I could talk to you about something your daughter told me. I brought food." She held up the open bag, displaying the muffins and the sandwiches tantalisingly wrapped in semi-transparent paper.

The woman only hesitated long enough to glance at the meat slurry on people's plates before saying, "Ok, let's go."

They found a low wall edging a flagstone walkway and sat down next to each other, the bag of food between them. Holly handed over a diet coke and then pulled out both sandwiches.

"I brought one brie and pear and one ham and cheddar.

You can have whichever you want."

She opted for the brie and pear and was immediately raised in Holly's estimation. They both tucked into their sandwiches with gusto and for a time they were silent except for the sound of chewing and occasional noise of appreciation. Once she was nearing the end of her sandwich the nurse took a sip of coke and turned slightly to face towards Holly.

"So, how do you know my daughter?" she asked.

It wasn't the question that Holly had expected but she supposed that it should have been.

"I catered a dinner at the weekend and she was serving the food," Holly explained.

"Ah! You're the cook! Lydia was very impressed. I hope you're not here to tell me that she did something awful," Mrs Pearsons said.

"No, no, nothing like that," Holly assured her, "It's just that she said something interesting and I was hoping that you could explain it."

The woman was looking at her warily now and Holly wasn't sure how to continue.

"Mrs Pearsons..."

"Lisa."

"Thank you, Lisa... I understand that you were working the night Debbie Hall died."

Holly saw a door close behind her companion's eyes. She wasn't prepared to talk about this subject and Holly wasn't sure whether she could persuade her to change her mind. Lisa took another bite of her sandwich and didn't say anything at all. Holly decided to keep going, maybe if she was careful the woman would open up a little.

"I'm not going to ask you to tell me anything you're not comfortable with, and definitely nothing that you can't legally tell me."

Now Lisa looked at her, "I'm not sure what that leaves."

Holly wasn't really sure either. "No, good point. But hopefully it leaves something that can help me."

"Need it for a new recipe do you?" Lisa cast her withering look and Holly couldn't help but flinch. What was she doing here?

"I need to know if there's a connection to Terry Wood." She just blurted it out and immediately regretted it. She'd felt the situation slipping out of her control but she wished that she'd led into her real question more carefully. Lisa was now looking at her with suspicion and alarm, and Holly couldn't think of any way to back-pedal. The question was out there and Holly just had to wait. They sat there for another minute in silence and Holly contemplated tipping herself backwards off the wall, crawling away and pretending that this had never happened, but she was glad that she didn't.

"Terry Wood is really dead, right?" Lisa asked eventually.

"Yes, he is," Holly confirmed.

"I saw it in the paper, it said that it was him and that they found him in the woods but it didn't say much else."

"My dad found him when he was out walking the dog," Holly told her.

"So that's your interest in all this is it?" Lisa asked

astutely.

"Pretty much. And... just... someone died," Holly added, not sure how to explain.

"Everybody dies. Terry Wood is no loss. Are you really telling me he'll be missed?" They were harsh words but for the most part Holly wasn't sure she disagreed. Some people had cared about Terry though.

"He had friends," Holly argued.

"I doubt that very much. And besides, it doesn't outweigh the bad he did," Lisa countered.

"Are you talking about Debbie?" Holly asked.

"She was only a few years older than my Lydia. I'll never forget her parents that night," Lisa went abruptly quiet. They had strayed too close to topics that she wasn't prepared to discuss.

"Was Terry involved though? I know that he sold drugs, it seems like most people knew it, but that doesn't mean that he's the one who sold the drugs to Debbie Hall," Holly probed.

"It was him. He was in the car with her. He was brought in in the same ambulance, barely a scratch on him. He was supposed to get checked out by a doctor but he left before anyone saw him. He just walked away. She died and he just walked away. How is that fair?" Lisa asked, her gaze intense.

"Are you sure?!" Holly asked. If this was true it would mean that Debbie Hall could definitely be a motive for Terry's murder.

"He wasn't mentioned in any of the newspaper articles,"

she added.

"He didn't give his name to the EMTs or to the hospital when he got here. Then, like I said, he just left. No one even asked about him, he got missed in the shuffle. I mentioned it to the police but Debbie had been the one driving and they just didn't seem interested in whether she had anyone with her," Lisa explained.

Holly thought for a moment. She wished that she had her notebook with her so that she could get it all down on paper and ease the pressure on her overcrowded brain. There was still something that she needed to know. "Did anyone else know that Terry Wood had been in the car? That he had sold her the drugs?"

Lisa was looking at her very intensely now. She was no fool and she had certainly figured out why Holly was asking. Holly could more than understand her reluctance to answer, but she needed to know.

"Someone's been murdered Lisa. It's important. Besides, I'm not the police remember, I'm just a baker. What's the harm in telling me?"

Chapter 17

An hour later Holly was sat in her flat with an empty mug beside her, her fingers smudged with ink and two more pages of her notebook filled. Lisa had admitted that Debbie Hall's father had seen Terry Wood at the hospital. There was no guarantee that Mr Hall would have known who Terry was, but if he had recognised him and knew that he was a drug dealer then you could pretty much guarantee that he would have made the connection between Terry and Debbie's death. This meant that Holly was going to have to go and see Mr Hall. She'd been hoping to avoid this. Of every potential suspect he was the one who had most reason to kill Terry and he was the one that, as grieving father, Holly felt least deserved to go to prison for the crime. She knew that that wasn't how the justice system worked but she couldn't help but hope that a villain in a black cape would sweep out of the shadows and prove guilty of Terry's murder.

Holly decided to push everything aside for now. She wasn't ready to talk to Mr Hall so it would just have to wait. She was going to make a plan and think out what to say and in the meantime she wanted some friendly faces. The promise of samples should be enough to get her an invite to her parents' house. The peanut butter cups were perfect and the muffins didn't need much work, so Holly decided that she would make a fresh batch of the strawberry bars with a few changes, and take some of the granola bars as they were. She knew they needed work but it would still help to get feedback now. Holly called her mother to check that they were home and happy for her to come over and then she got to work. She added lemon zest to the strawberry slice base this time, and a tiny bit of cinnamon. Fighting the urge to sugar the strawberries, she popped them into the oven and packed up her stuff to go while they baked. She grabbed her laptop as well as the usual phone and keys. She could start on the calorie calculations at her parents' house. Whipping up a quick glaze, she poured it into a Tupperware pot to take with her and then slid the still hot strawberry slices into an open tin. They could cool down on the drive.

Holly pulled onto her parents' driveway with a sigh of relief. Would it ever stop feeling like coming home? Her father was watering the pots by the front door and he set down the watering can and came forward, smiling, to help her with her things. He carried the tin inside, lifting it to his face to breathe in the smell of warm, fresh cooked strawberries. He set them down on the dining table in the conservatory and Holly set down the tray with the rest of the samples beside it.

"To what do we owe this smorgasbord of delights?"

"I'm developing healthy recipes for the Leisure Centre Cafe," Holly explained.

"Well you know I'm always more than happy to provide feedback," her father responded, rubbing his hands together.

"Is that my darling daughter with some cakes?" Maggie called out as she came in from the garden. She entered the conservatory just as her husband reached out for a peanut butter cup and was only just in time to slap his hand away.

"Het hem. What do you think you're doing? A proper tasting like this calls for cups of tea to cleanse the palette!" Maggie declared.

"Of course my love! What was I thinking?! Your wish is my command!"

As Holly watched her father bow his way out of the room and into the kitchen, she felt a wave of loneliness. She wanted what her parents had. She wanted the camaraderie and the ease of conversation. She wanted someone who would know when she was joking. She wanted someone to always be there.

"The police called," her mother's anxious voice broke her out of her little pit of self indulgence.

"What?"

"The police, they want him to go in to the station again tomorrow to talk to them. They said they won't keep him long but what if they do?! Why do they want to talk to him again?!" Maggie was speaking at break neck speed and glancing towards the kitchen. Holly suspected that her father had told her not to tell their daughter. The fact that she would ignore the request was a testament to just how worried Maggie really was.

"It'll be alright mum, I promise. The police seem to be

just asking people about drugs. They're trying to find out who Terry was dealing to. Dad has nothing to do with anything like that so he'll be fine," Holly tried to reassure her mother and herself at the same time.

"But what if they think that he did?! What if they think that's why your father was in the woods?!"

Damn. That was a very good point.

"In that case we'll call Dan. In fact, if I have to I'll go to London and drag Dan back here myself to sort the whole thing out. Dad didn't do anything wrong. He'll be fine."

That was all they had time for before Richard returned carrying a tray laden with mugs of tea, and they had to quickly affix smiles to their faces.

"Lovely Dad, thank you! Right, everyone try the granola bars first please."

Over multiple cups of tea they munched their way through a substantial portion of what Holly had brought with her. They decided that the peanut butter cups were indeed perfect just as they were. The muffins were lovely, they just needed a certain something but they weren't sure what it was. The granola bars could do with something tangy. The warm, nutty, honey flavours were wonderful but a tangy flavour somewhere would balance them out. Holly thought that maybe she'd try dried cranberries or maybe dried bitter cherries. The strawberry slices with their new adaptations went down a treat but they all much preferred them with the glaze. Holly explained about the calorie counting and her father was interested in it from a scientific perspective but her mother was utterly opposed.

"I don't want to know the calories of every indulgence! I want to enjoy my food, not feel bad about it!" she exclaimed.

"Well that's the point mum. A lot of people going to the gym wouldn't eat something like this at all, but if they see a low calorie count then they might eat it and enjoy it and that would be lovely! You should have seen Jack's face when he tried the peanut butter cup, they were his favourite before he started at the gym and he hasn't eaten one in years!" Holly explained.

"Well that's just sad! That poor young man should have been eating peanut butter cups!"

"But I don't think he would have enjoyed them, knowing how unhealthy they were," Holly suggested. It wasn't a thought process that she could completely understand, but she could sympathise from a distance. Holly had always enjoyed food. She liked cooking it and she liked eating it and her slightly soft waistline reflected this. She'd never been fat but she certainly didn't have a sleek, toned gym body either.

"Well I'm glad you're not like that sweetheart, there's no harm in enjoying food. It's good to have a bit of meat on you," Holly felt these encouraging words to be at odds with the somewhat sympathetic pat on the shoulder that accompanied them. She and her mother both looked up at Richard in mingled incredulity and rage and he, sensing danger, fled to his study to work on his painting.

Maggie looked at her daughter with concern, "Men are idiots. You know that, don't you? You're beautiful."

"I love you mum," Holly fiddled with the mug in her

hands, turning it back and forth "Do you ever wish that I was more girly?"

"What do you mean darling?"

"Well I know you always wanted a girl, and I never did all the make-up and high heels stuff. I just wondered if you were..." Holly trailed off, not wanting to finish the thought.

"Disappointed?" To Holly's great relief her mother sounded amused "Darling you are exactly the child I wished for. And besides, what makes you think I wanted a girl?"

Holly looked at her mother in confusion.

"Well you had three boys and you kept trying... I just assumed you were trying to have a girl."

Maggie laughed. "Really, I just loved having babies! I liked the idea of a big family and once we'd had a couple it was already chaos and I just didn't want to stop! I was never happier then when all you little ones were playing and shouting. You'll see."

"So I'm not too much of a tom-boy for you?" Holly asked.

"Goodness grief no! I feel lucky to have escaped your teen years without having to deal with miniskirts and heels! You're my perfect girl darling, I'm so proud of you," Maggie told her sincerely.

Holly marvelled at the fact that her mother always seemed to know what to say to make her feel better.

"Besides, I was bound to be a tom-boy with all those dogs and three older brothers," Holly suggested.

"You weren't always a tom-boy dear. I wouldn't even say you are one now really, you're just not fussed about clothes and things. You were when you were little though, you started picking out your own clothes when you were two and you wore some brilliant outfits! You kept it up for at least a few years too. You looked wonderful!" Maggie assured her.

"Really? A two year old dressing themselves doesn't sound like it would be a fashion marvel," Holly suggested, chuckling.

Her mother leapt to her feet and dashed from the room, returning a few minutes later with a navy blue, leather bound photo album clutched in her hands. She laid it before her daughter triumphantly.

Holly opened it to the first page and found her own young face staring back at her defiantly. Chin raised, eyes fiery, hair wild, she was sporting a bright red jumper with pink bobbles all over it, a blue skirt, red tights and pink and yellow striped wellington boots. She was a riot of colour and energy and that turned out to be the overriding theme throughout the album. There was the odd picture of her tiny form clad in floral pyjamas or white nighties but mostly she was wearing rainbow jumpers, patterned tights, sparkly everything and fairy wings. No one colour seemed to be represented more than any other, it was a beautiful mishmash. The fairy wings appeared again and again and her mother explained that she had got them for her third birthday and worn them almost every day for about a year. It rang a small tinkling bell in the recesses of Holly's mind but she couldn't quite picture it in the first person. It was more like she was remembering hearing about it in later years. She couldn't remember being that little girl in the colourful clothing.

Maggie pointed to a photo of Holly in a knitted rainbow jumper, a denim skirt, yellow tights and wellies, "When I see that picture I can remember exactly what you felt like. My baby girl in that jumper, it was so soft. It was one of your favourites, you wore it all the time and it just takes me right back when I see it. My mother knitted that for you. You're so much like her."

Maggie's tone was wistful and Holly looked at her mother eagerly. Her grandmother had passed away when she was only five and she didn't remember much about her. She had hazy recollections of silky dresses, lavender perfume, fresh baked cookies and looking for fairies in the garden, but it had all taken on a slightly fairytale feel and Holly wasn't sure how accurate her memories were. She couldn't remember the sound of her grandmother's voice and when she pictured her face it was always photos, but she knew that she had been loved and that her grandmother had been a wonderful woman. Seeing her daughter's expression, Maggie seemed to understand how her daughter felt.

"I wish you'd had more time with her darling. But she loved you so much."

"I know. I think I remember baking with her when I was little," Holly told her.

"Oh yes, you two were always creating things. There were endless varieties of your fairy biscuits."

"Fairy biscuits?" Holly asked.

Maggie laughed, "You used to make biscuits together to

give to the fairies in the garden, though I think you always ended up eating them all! Sometimes you would put in peanut butter, sometimes chocolate, sometimes sprinkles, or jam or sometimes something crazy like marmite. I think you did some with olives in once! You told me you were trying to find what food the fairies liked. You said if you found the right one then the fairies would come out and get the biscuits and you could see one," Maggie told her.

Holly smiled at the thought. She wished that she could remember it but it was still a wonderful story.

"That sounds lovely. Did I ever see one?" she asked.

"A fairy?" her mother laughed, "no, but you didn't mind. It was an adventure. That's what my mother was like, she made everything fun. It just mattered that you got to believe."

"It sounds like she was amazing. I always remember her as being a bit magical. I don't think I inherited that from her at all. I'm probably the least magical person there is," Holly admitted regretfully.

"You inherited her love of baking, her love of food and her love of nature. You have her energy inside you and her joy in making other people happy. You do wonderful things with your cooking darling, if that's not magic I don't know what is."

Holly smiled at her mother and gave her a hug. It was a wonderful thing to be a part of a family. The thought reminded her of her father's impending visit to the police. She couldn't believe that anyone could really think that her father would be out in the woods meeting with drug dealers, but the fact they had asked him to come in and speak to them indicated the police were at least considering the possibility. Hard as it was going to be, Holly was going to need to go and see Michael Hall. If she could figure out whether or not he knew about Terry's drug dealing then she could rule him in or out as a suspect. She had the name of the construction company he managed, she could track him down the following afternoon.

Chapter 18

Holly was back to sleeping fretfully that night, but the following morning she awoke focused and fuelled by purpose. Her regular baking and deliveries seemed to pass in a matter of moments. She functioned on autopilot, her mind running through what she needed to accomplish and how she might go about it. She settled on the loose makings of a plan and then, once back at her flat, she began to set it in motion. Taking out some of her muffin tins and pulling ingredients toward her, she set about assembling her basic cake mix. Separating out half she added vanilla and lemon zest to one half and cocoa and espresso to the other. Once she'd filled a couple of trays of paper cases with the two cake mixes she slid them into the oven and started on her buttercream. They wouldn't be the fanciest cupcakes in the world but Holly knew that even her basic sponge cake mix was delicious and the cupcakes would serve their purpose admirably. She had a vanilla buttercream and a chocolate buttercream all ready to go before the cakes were cool enough to top. Put buttercream onto a warm cake and you end up with less of a beautiful swirl of icing and more of a puddle of icing. Holly decided to use the cake cooling time to make herself a cup of tea and

a couple of slices of cheese on toast. She realised that it was
not the day to skip a meal, she wanted to be at her best to
talk to Mr Hall and that meant not having an empty stomach.
By the time she'd consumed this simple repast the cakes
were just about cool enough. She quickly topped each of
them with a neat twist of buttercream, put half in a tin and
half into one of the white cardboard boxes that she used
when people ordered cupcakes from her directly, rather than
buying them from one of the cafes. She slipped a couple of
her business cards into the box and set off.

A quick internet search had informed her that J.H.
Construction was currently working on a small, new
development on the edge of town. She wasn't sure if this was
where Michael Hall would be, but she suspected that it
would at least be a good place to start her search. It was
another warm day and Holly sincerely hoped that she found
Mr Hall quickly, the buttercream would be much happier
indoors out of the heat. Climbing out of her van, Holly
balanced the large cupcake box in one hand and grabbed her
bag with the other. The development looked as though it was
going to be a small collection of flats and houses with a
courtyard in the middle. It looked as though it was going to
turn out to be very nice, but if Holly were going to move
she'd want it to be to somewhere with a garden. There were
lots of people here working, far more than Holly had
expected, but she didn't think that the boss would be
operating a digger or laying bricks. Off to one side were a
couple of temporary structures emblazoned with the J.H.
Construction logo and it was towards these that Holly

headed. She noted with chagrin that in her walking boots, jeans and t-shirt she didn't look at all out of place. All she needed was a hi-vis vest and a hard hat and she could get straight to work. It was definitely time to go shopping.

The two temporary structures were joined together, and reaching the first Holly found it to be an antechamber of sorts. There was a reception desk currently staffed by a cheerful looking woman with a neat blonde bob, a low table set towards one side with four low chairs around it and pictures of beautiful homes decorated in shades of magnolia all over the walls. Holly confidently bounced up to the secretary behind the desk and asked for Mr Michael Hall. The secretary's eyes darted to the door behind her but she smilingly refused.

"I'm so sorry, Mr Hall is currently very busy, can I ask what it's regarding? If you're hoping to purchase one of the beautiful properties currently under construction outside then I am more than happy to direct you to the correct team to handle your request."

The cheerful professionalism was daunting but Holly was not to be dissuaded.

"No, thank you, I'm not currently in the market, I was just hoping for two minutes of Mr Hall's time. I have some cake samples for him and they won't last long on a beautiful day like today". Holly beamed at the secretary, knowing herself to have scored a point. Not many bosses would be happy to have free cake refused on their behalf and it seemed that neither would Mr Hall. The secretary smiled grudgingly and went to the door behind her. Stepping through it she closed it behind her for just a moment before coming back out to her desk and sending Holly in.

"There better be cake for me!" she called out good naturedly, half to Holly and half to Mr Hall, who welcomed Holly with a handshake and a curious look.

"So, what's all this about cake? I don't think I've ordered anything."

"No, no, this is a free sample. I run a small baked goods company and I like to give samples to local business owners in case they ever host any events that need catering. I can provide cakes for birthdays, office parties, other events... I also cater formal functions but that's harder to provide samples of." Holly gave her little speech followed by a friendly smile and was pleased to see that Mr Hall appeared to accept the explanation happily.

"Well I'm always happy to accept free samples! If you leave them with me and give me a card then we'll definitely bear you in mind for any future events." He held out a hand expectantly and Holly handed over the box of cakes. She had planned for this possibility.

"Here are the cakes, there's chocolate and vanilla. I've put a couple of copies of my business card in the box. I would really love it if you'd try one of the cakes now. I don't want to impose too much on your time but I find that if the boss doesn't try one of the cakes right away they get too busy and forget. I'm more than happy for your workforce to get a treat but if you don't try one I'm much less likely to get any future business out of it." It was a blatant sales pitch and made Holly cringe internally but she needed to buy herself more time to get him talking. She smiled at him hopefully and he chuckled in response. Michael Hall was a big man, physically he would be more than capable of killing a man with a rock but looking at him Holly still found that she couldn't picture it. If she had been hoping for a stereotypical villain, Michael Hall wasn't it. He looked like a nice, normal, all be it tired man, with tanned skin, blue eyes and a face crinkled with smile lines.

He opened the box and looked at the beautiful cakes. The scent of sugar and chocolate filled the room and he smiled up at Holly appreciatively.

"These look great! Are you sure they're free?" He looked mock teasing and Holly laughed before reassuring him.

"Absolutely! Just bear me in mind for any future events that you might host! I can do private events too, do you live locally?" Holly asked casually.

Michael Hall's hands danced through the air above the open box, carefully selecting a cake to try. He lifted a chocolate cupcake and answered briefly before taking a bite. "Oh yes, I've lived in this town my whole life." He then sunk his teeth into the sponge and buttercream and sighed with contentment.

"Me too," Holly responded, "I love it here. It's such a great place to live. Though there was that awful murder last week, did you hear about it?"

Mr Hall looked up at her with his mouth full of cake and gave a half nod.

"Sorry," Holly continued, "That's a really tactless thing

to ask, you might have known him, and then here I am asking about it casually, as though it's just a talking point."

Michael Hall had finished his mouthful and laughed gently, "No, don't worry."

Holly waited a beat before asking, in what she hoped was a casual voice, "No I haven't offended you? Or no, you didn't know him?"

Mr Hall was no longer quite looking at ease. Years of social awkwardness meant that Holly was used to this, but still it was a shame.

"I read about it in the paper but I don't think I know the fellow. It was a young man I think, not really in my social circle," Mr Hall explained.

"Terence Wood. Terry. He was in his twenties," Holly stated.

"Oh, did you know him then?" Mr Hall asked.

"Not really," Holly answered, "He went to my school but wasn't in my year."

"Well it's very sad at any rate," Mr Hall offered in an offhand way. He certainly didn't seem as though he was discussing a man he had recently murdered. He hadn't reacted to Terry's name being mentioned and he didn't seem nervous. If anything he seemed to be wondering why this mad young woman was standing in front of him discussing murders and forcing him to eat cake while she watched.

"Yes. Very sad," Holly finished lamely. "So what did you think of the chocolate?"

Clearly relieved at the change in conversation Michael Hall's face broke out into a wide smile.

"I think it was so good that I'm definitely trying a vanilla one too!"

With that he reached into the box and drew out one of the pale, creamy cakes and took a huge bite, again sighing with pleasure. Holly could almost never resist going for the chocolate when it was available but she knew that her vanilla buttercream was a real treat. The vanilla flavour really came through despite the sweetness and it was light as air after being whipped up into clouds of sugary froth. The vanilla cake went down just as well as the chocolate and before she left Holly was gratified to see Mr Hall fish one of her business cards out of the box and pin it to his notice board. He followed Holly out of his office and gave the box with the remaining cupcakes to his secretary.

"You can have one Trish, and then maybe you could think of a way to allocate the rest fairly to the guys?"

"Thank you!" the woman replied, "I'll use them as a little reward scheme today I think. See if I can get everyone moving a bit faster."

"With these cakes as an incentive we could have finished work by the end of the day!" Michael was still laughing to himself as Holly waved a final goodbye from the doorway and headed out.

She knew that it wasn't concrete but Michael Hall did not seem like a murderer. He would have to be very cold-blooded indeed to bash a man's head in with a rock and then calmly sit and chat about him with a complete stranger. He might have prepared himself for questions from friends or family, or maybe even from the police, but someone that he didn't know catching him off guard with a mention of Terry? Surely that would elicit some kind of reaction. Michael Hall had appeared calm and totally uninterested in the death of Terry Wood. Holly couldn't help but feel relieved even though it left her back at square one.

Chapter 19

Once she was back at her flat Holly gave her mum a quick call. Maggie informed her that her father had been at the police station for a couple of hours earlier in the day and hadn't said much about it since arriving home. Holly asked if she could come for dinner again and promised to bring some unhealthy treats this time as a contribution to the meal. She wanted to know why the police had been talking to her father again and she was hoping that he'd have some insight into the direction their investigation was taking. Holly might have hit a dead end but that didn't mean that her interest was over.

Her mother greeted her at the door with a grateful expression and Holly could tell that she was worried.

"How's dad? Has he said anything more?" Holly asked.

"No," Maggie shook her head, "He still hasn't really told me what they asked him or even why they wanted him to come back in to see them. Do you think he's a suspect?"

Holly was pretty sure that the police wouldn't be wasting time having her father in for questioning if he *wasn't* a suspect but she couldn't come out and say that to her mother.

"Even if he is, he won't be for long. Once they find out

what happened and who's actually responsible, it'll be obvious that dad had nothing to do with it." Holly spoke much more confidently than she felt but it had the desired effect. Her mother visibly relaxed and smiled, pulling her daughter in for a hug.

"You're right darling. Of course you are. Now, what's in the tin?" Maggie asked excitedly.

Her mother oohed and aahd at the cupcakes admiringly and they set them in the cool of the kitchen.

"So, where is Dad?" Holly looked around but couldn't see her father concealed anywhere.

"He's out in the garden pottering. Maybe you could take him a cup of tea and see if you can get any information out of him. I'm starting dinner but it'll be a little while, I'm making risotto."

Holly set about making three large mugs of tea and then placed one on the kitchen counter near her mother. Clutching the handles of the two remaining mugs in one hand she checked that her mother wasn't looking and snuck a couple of cupcakes from the tin with her free hand before slipping out the back door into the garden.

In the garden, her father's domain was down towards the end. They hadn't focused on this stretch while Holly had been growing up, instead letting the plants that were already there run wild while they prioritised the flower beds that lined the lawn and the patio up by the house. The way her father told it, when he had retired he had ventured through the rose arch at the bottom of the garden for the first time in years and found his new purpose in life. The fact that he had found his purpose in stained glass, oil painting, furniture restoration and a whole host of other vocations had not in any way diminished his excitement. He had cut back and weeded and cleared and planted and had eventually created a haphazard but beautiful vegetable garden. Some of the plants and shrubs that were there were happy and healthy and Richard Abbot hadn't wanted to uproot them. This meant that instead of neat rows of plants, there were meandering lines of lettuces and potatoes interspersed with Echinacea, bushes of salvia and huge, great hydrangeas. While he still jumped from project to project, Holly's father kept up his garden with care and diligence. Holly now found him bent over, weeding around his rosemary plant. He looked up as she approached and smiled.

"Hello love! I didn't realise we were having the pleasure of your company today."

"Mum said I could come for dinner," Holly explained. "I brought some cakes."

"Well you know you're always welcome," His eyes travelled to the cupcakes in her hand, "As are your cakes!" .

Once her father had extricated a cup of tea from her grip and one of the cakes to go with it, they both sat down on the low, grubby stools that lived down the end of the garden for Richard and Maggie to perch on while planting. They sipped their tea and ate their cakes in silence for a few minutes, Holly just enjoying spending a peaceful moment with her father. After all that had happened over the past few days it was nice to see him here, pottering about in the garden, exactly where he belonged. It was still inconceivable to

Holly that someone could believe this gentle, creative man could be capable of doing anyone harm.

"Dad?"

"Yes love?"

"Why did the police have you back in to talk to them again?" she asked him gently.

He sighed deeply before answering,

"They just had some more questions," he told her.

Holly waited for him to continue but it became increasingly clear as the seconds ticked by that he felt he'd explained sufficiently.

"Dad, Mum's worried. Were they asking about Terry's drug dealing?" she probed.

Her father looked up at her quickly and she hastened to reassure him,

"I didn't know about it first-hand! But Terry went to my school remember. Everyone knew he sold drugs," she told him.

Richard sighed again. "Well that says something very sad about the state of the school. I'm really glad that I retired." He took a couple more sips of tea before continuing.

"Yes, they were asking about drugs. They wanted to know if I was aware of Terence's drug dealing and if I had ever bought drugs from him or supplied him with drugs." He looked sad and embarrassed and Holly knew how these questions must have hurt a man of his good reputation and strong sense of morality.

"They want to know if you supplied him with drugs?! What do they think this is?! Breaking bad?!" Holly was outraged and scared for her father. He chuckled at her joke but he too looked scared.

"I wasn't able to tell them much of anything and I think they suspected that I was being purposefully unhelpful. There were always rumours in school amongst the teachers, but I don't even know if Terence was still involved in anything like that," he told her.

"He was," Holly confirmed. "He's done a few other odd jobs but he was still selling drugs and none of his legitimate jobs lasted long."

"Well you're better informed than me, my love. Possibly better informed than the police at this point. They didn't mention anywhere that Terence had worked or really anything about him at all. They were very focused on narcotics. I suppose it makes sense, if a drug dealer gets killed it will almost certainly be related to drugs, but it was very sad to hear a human life reduced to such a simple, grubby strand. I would hope that there was more to Terence's life than just that one aspect."

Gosh, Richard Abbot was a wonderful man. Holly loved her father and his unceasing ability to shift the world back to a bigger, more beautiful picture. In this case other aspects of Terry's life included theft from the elderly, but it was a nice idea. Maybe there was more to Terry than Holly kept hearing. She couldn't imagine Joe being friends with someone like Terry so maybe there was a side to him that she needed to know more about.

Holly gave her father a quick kiss on the cheek before she headed back up to the house to see if her mother needed any help with dinner. She called back over her shoulder as she went, "Don't tell Mum about the cakes, she's making risotto!"

As she walked back into the kitchen her mother asked, "How is he? I take it you're both full of cake now? You better not have ruined your appetites, I've got a huge pot of risotto here!"

Ah well, best laid plans an d all that.

Holly actually didn't feel particularly hungry right up until her mother brought the risotto to the table and took the lid off of the pot. The rich creamy rice was a warm yellow colour and was interspersed with jewel bright vegetables. The smell was incredible and teamed as it was with fresh bread spread liberally with salty butter, safe to say Holly and her father both made excellent meals. Even once they were full to bursting, they both managed a small coffee and another cake each before finally leaning back in their chairs, sated and sleepy. They filled the rest of the evening with light chatter. Holly told them more about her plans to offer healthy options to some of her other existing customers. Her father discussed second-hand sales he wanted to go to, to hunt down old furniture pieces to upcycle. Maggie told them snippets about the next book that she was planning, another bodice ripper but this time set in a new, sunny location that would probably need to be researched first hand in order to lend it authenticity. Once she'd had her fill of watching her parents bicker affectionately about Maggie's desire for a holiday and Richard's reluctance to leave his garden unattended, Holly headed back to her flat. It felt all the more cold and depressing after an evening spent in the warm and comforting embrace of her family home and Holly resolved once again to put some effort into personalising the space soon.

Chapter 20

Holly slept well after an evening of good food and wonderful company but when she woke to the sound of her alarm, her first thought was of her father. Could the police really suspect him of any wrong doing? Dan had never worked with the local police and so Holly didn't know if she could trust them. If they were all complete idiots then her father could be dragged through a harrowing ordeal of suspicion before the whole thing got sorted out.

More than ever Holly wanted to figure out who was responsible and clear her father's name but what avenue was there left to explore? Having spoken to Michael Hall she didn't think that he was guilty. He had been her best and only suspect and without him Holly wasn't clear on where to go from here. Resolving to put it out of her mind for the time being, Holly dragged herself from the comfort of her bed to start the day. She determined that she would be focused and organised and would concentrate on work until she had completed her deliveries for the day and then she would sit down and give the matter some dedicated thought. It was a nice plan, but organised as she had hoped to be, she still forgot her towel on the way to the bathroom.

It had become such a fixed routine that Holly could complete her morning food preparations on autopilot. She felt like she woke from a daydream to find herself loading the van, ready to hit the road. While her hands had been mixing, stirring and assembling, her mind had been hard at work and Holly felt as though there was an idea at the edge of her subconscious that she couldn't quite grasp. A few details that she had learned were starting to make a picture but there were still gaps. Large portions of the whole were still missing and Holly couldn't quite bring it into focus without them. Frustrated and confused she again pushed it to the back of her mind and set off to deliver her orders.

Safely ensconced back in her flat a couple of hours later, Holly made herself a huge mug of tea and a couple of pieces of cheese and pickle on toast. Sitting down on the sofa she got comfortable, took a bite of toast and opened her notebook. She started by reading through everything that she had written down so far. She had pages of information on everyone involved, pages on her conversations with them and pages of seemingly disconnected thoughts and ideas. It was apparent that her later conversations had elicited pages and pages of writing, whereas her early attempts had only resulted in a few measly lines. Pierce, Joe and Sandra all warranted talking to again. She was so nervous when she spoke to them that she'd barely asked them any questions at all. Pierce had seemed content to talk to her but hadn't had much to tell, but Sandra had seemed to be equal parts aggressive and clueless and Holly had felt as though they were speaking different languages. Even her talks with Joe had been vague and uncomfortable. Holly was so afraid of offending people that she was tiptoeing around the issues she actually wanted to discuss.

Finishing off her toast, her tea long since gone, Holly decided to start with Joe. She'd already talked to him a couple of times but she had the advantage of a built-in excuse. Holly had been at the youth centre just a few days prior to cater the dinner, she could stick a spatula or something in her bag and say that she was there looking for it. There was no conceivable reason why Holly would ever be at the horse riding school so Sandra would be a more complicated visit, and short of sabotaging her van she didn't have a reason to see Pierce either. No, definitely easier to start with Joe Dawkins and see if there was anything more that she could learn from him.

Once the plate and mug were cleared away and the last traces of crumbs were washed off her hands, it was time to go. At the last moment Holly remembered her plan and put a whisk into her bag to take with her. She drove to the youth centre fine, walked in no problem, found the kitchen without issue... then stopped. If she was really there to find her missing whisk then surely at this point she would locate the utensil and then go. The realisation that her plan was a total dud hit her in a wave and she let out a sound somewhere between an exasperated sigh, a snort and a giggle that she was sincerely glad no one was around to hear.

"Holly?"

She spun round to find Joe standing in the doorway of

the kitchen looking slightly alarmed. Great. He had probably heard the weird noise she'd made and was now wondering what on earth was wrong with her.

"Oh, hi Joe," Holly smiled and tried to look like a normal person, not one sneaking around making weird noises in kitchens.

"What are you doing here?" It was a fair question but for a moment Holly panicked. Her mind went completely blank and all she could do was stare at Joe with her mouth open and will words to come out. Finally, in a rush, she remembered her plan.

"My whisk!" So excited was she to have remembered her plan and actually vocalised something that she practically shouted it. Joe took a half step back, presumably in case she had totally lost her mind and become dangerous, so Holly hastened to explain at a more moderate volume.

"I left my whisk here on Saturday. When I catered the meal I must have put it away with the youth centre's stuff or maybe dropped it somewhere. I thought I would come and look for it," she told him.

"Well we can't have that! Let me help you look. What does it look like?" he asked.

"Thanks Joe, it has a dark blue handle."

With that they both moved further into the kitchen and started opening and closing cupboards and drawers, hunting for the whisk that at that moment was comfortably nestled in Holly's bag between her mobile phone and her notebook. The longer they searched, the more Holly realised that it would be almost impossible to sneak the whisk out of her bag and pretend to find it somewhere. The kitchen wasn't exactly huge and they had searched almost the whole place within a couple of minutes. Where could Holly say she had found it and what if Joe saw her take it out of her bag? Wishing that she'd never mentioned the whisk in the first place, Holly decided to just bite the bullet.

"Joe?"

He looked up at her enquiringly from where he was knelt down looking under the washing machine.

"Joe, can I ask you a few more questions about Terry Wood?"

"What questions are those?" He didn't look at all happy about it but at least he wasn't saying no.

"Why did you recommend him for jobs? Why were you friends with him? It seems like you're the only person who was, and I wanted to know if there was another side to him that other people weren't aware of."

Joe sighed, "I just thought he deserved a chance is all. He was young, he made mistakes, lots of people do. People make mistakes but it shouldn't ruin their whole lives, that's not fair."

He was so sincere and impassioned, Holly wondered if Terry had known how lucky he was to have Joe in his corner. Joe was the sort of person who would do anything for the people he cared about.

"Did you know that he was selling drugs? To teenagers at the youth centre."

Joe was looking stricken now. For a moment it looked as though he couldn't speak. Holly wondered at the whorl of emotions in his eyes.

"Would I have let him come round here if I knew that?" Joe sounded bitter and hurt and Holly felt a pang at having to cause him pain like this. "Do you have any more questions for me?"

"The day he died, Terry came here in the afternoon. Had you arranged the visit? Why did he come?"

Joe thought before responding, "Yes, I was working here and couldn't get out for long to meet up so we arranged between us for him to come by. Just for a chat though, nothing special."

"And he definitely came on his bike?" she asked.

"What?"

"His bike, did he definitely cycle here?"

"You asked about that before, I don't understand why it matters," he told her.

"No, I'm not sure I do either," Holly admitted.

Joe sighed again, "Yes, he came on his bike and he left on his bike. I have no idea where his bike is. Holly, why are you asking all this?"

Now it was Holly's turn to sigh. "The police have been questioning my dad. He found the body and he knew Terry, they had problems when my dad was still teaching. Now they're asking my dad about drugs, wanting to know if he'd ever bought or sold drugs to Terry. I'm really worried about him!" Holly hadn't planned on saying so much or ending on that impassioned little cry and she noted uncomfortably that Joe looked genuinely horrified.

"They can't! They can't think your dad had anything to

do with this can they?! He was always such a nice bloke, always had a chat when he was picking you and your brothers up from stuff. He's such a quiet guy and so nice... they can't! He hasn't done anything wrong!"

Rather than making her feel vindicated, hearing her own thoughts echoed back at her was just making Holly feel a bit queasy. Worry for her father was starting to feel like a very heavy load.

"I don't know Joe. I know he didn't do anything wrong but they've made it clear that they suspect him," she told him.

"What about the person he was going to meet?" Joe asked quickly.

Holly looked at Joe intensely, this was something new and possibly very helpful.

"What do you mean? You didn't say anything about this before, who was he going to meet? Where was he going?" Holly asked eagerly.

"Well, I don't know. I mean, he didn't tell me details but he said he was going to meet someone. A shady character from out of town. That couldn't be your father, could it? He's lived in this town practically his whole life!"

This was true. Holly's father couldn't be described as being from out of town. But it was such a vague description, how was she going to track this mystery individual down? With so little to go on, she suspected that even police resources wouldn't help if she had them.

"He didn't tell you a name? Or how he knew him maybe?" Holly was desperate for more information but Joe didn't have anything more for her than theorising.

"Maybe it was someone to do with the drugs? They found him in the woods didn't they? Why else would he be in the woods at night if not for some sort of drug deal?"

It was a good point. It always came back to that question, why was Terry in the woods in the first place? It was possible that it was all a drug deal gone bad and nothing to do with anyone from Holly's nice, safe world, but somehow Holly didn't think so. There was still a thought at the back of her brain that she couldn't put her finger on. Something that made her feel that if she could just hold all the details in her head at once that she would know exactly what had happened.

"Is there anything else Joe? Anything else at all that you can tell me?" Joe looked at her intensely, like there really was something else that he knew, something that he wasn't telling her. Holly tried to press the issue, "You were his friend Joe. Please, tell me."

A door closed behind Joe's eyes.

"Yes. I was his friend. If there was anything else I would tell you."

Chapter 21

Knowing that she wasn't going to get any further with Joe, Holly headed back to her flat. She updated her notes, made herself a quick dinner of pasta and salad and watched a couple of episodes of Miss Fisher's Murder Mysteries before heading to bed early. She didn't sleep well and when she woke she felt sluggish and heavy. She had to count through the days in her head to confirm that it was in fact Thursday and she didn't need to get up and frantically start baking. Instead she got up slowly, yawning her way to the bathroom. Allowing herself longer in the shower and conditioning her hair again made her feel a little better, but she wasn't truly revived until she had a plate of toast with jam and a huge mug of tea in front of her. She sat on the sofa in her comfiest clothes and munched her way through her toast whilst watching re-runs of Murder She Wrote. Holly had always enjoyed having Thursday as a weekly day off. The morning TV was eminently more to her liking than weekend viewing tended to be. She'd just started on an episode of Diagnosis Murder when her phone rang.

"Hello? Holly?"

She checked the caller ID, "Rebecca! Hello!"

"Ah, good, it is you. I just wanted to check that you'd received my invitation."

"Invitation?"

She heard Rebecca sigh down the phone, "Just as well I called. I sent you an invitation. It should be there! That is assuming that your mother gave me the correct address." Her tone implied that she doubted this very much but Holly climbed off the sofa and moved into the hall to search. Nothing was immediately apparent but wedged underneath the front mat, she found it: a postcard with a floral design on one side and her address on the other, as well as a brief missive begging the pleasure of her company for a family Sunday lunch.

"Arrive at twelve please. It should be a nice day so we'll all be eating out in the garden. You need to wear a dress. Not a fancy dress, it's not a formal do, but a summer dress."

"Well it's lovely of you to invite me Rebecca, but I won't know anyone. I might be busy..."

Holly hated herself for lying to her new friend and chickening out of a social event but she needn't have bothered with the self condemnation, Rebecca wasn't going to let her get away with it anyway.

"Of course you'll come. I checked with your mother and she told me that you don't work on Sundays. You can bring a cake."

And just like that she was gone. Holly held the silent phone to her ear for a minute, reeling from the social tornado that was a phone call with Rebecca Weiss.

Walking into her bedroom she threw the phone down on

top of the duvet and opened her wardrobe. She stared blindly at the shirts and t-shirts hanging inside for what felt like ages. Finally she had to admit to herself that however long she looked there still wouldn't be a dress in there. She retrieved her phone from the bed and dialled Kat's number.

"I need a dress suitable for a Sunday lunch garden party type thing." No preamble, this was an emergency and she needed help.

"Ok. What dresses do you have?" Bless Kat and her ability to pick up a conversational thread without any context or warm up.

"I have no dresses. I don't own any."

There was silence down the phone.

"Kat?"

"You literally don't own a single dress?"

"Kat! I need help!"

"When do you need it by?"

"This Sunday."

"Ok, What are you doing later today? We can go shopping."

"What about your work?"

"It's really quiet here today, the training that was scheduled got cancelled so we're all just drifting a bit. I'll ask my boss if I can leave a couple of hours early and make up the time next week."

Holly breathed a sigh of relief. What was she going to do without Kat?

"Thank you."

"I'll text you in a few minutes to confirm."

A couple of hours later Holly picked Kat up at her office and they drove straight to Cambridge. Holly was grateful to be able to focus on driving rather than the imminent task of shopping but Kat was overflowing with excitement. Practically bouncing up and down in her seat, Kat was running through various different styles, cuts and colours of summer dresses she had seen recently and then attempting to picture them on Holly and devise some sort of ranking system. She kept asking Holly if she thought that the creatively, and not always very clearly, described dresses sounded nice but Holly couldn't imagine anything looking good on herself. She knew that she was probably being silly but it had been so long since she'd worn a dress of any kind that it was starting to feel like a hurdle of ever increasing altitude. The more garments Kat described the more queasy Holly felt. By the time they found a space in the multi-story car park and made their way down to the shopping level, Holly had all but changed her mind about the whole thing.

Not for nothing had she and Kat been best friends for years. Taking one look at Holly's miserable face, Kat dragged her round the corner to an ice cream shop. It was one of those little independent places which only offers a few flavours but they all taste so incredible that you wonder why on earth you don't eat ice cream every single day of your life. With a sugared cone topped with a glossy, golden mound of honeycomb infused wonder in her hand Holly felt much better. Kat chose raspberry and rose and they enjoyed a few minutes of trying each other's flavour choice and then licking any stray rivulets caused by the balmy weather before continuing on their way.

"We won't be allowed to take the ice creams in any shops will we?"

"No," Kat confirmed, "But that's ok. Let's take a few minutes to stroll and you can point out any shops you like the look of. Just look at the clothes in the window and let me know if any look nice" She gave her friend a knowing look, "And I don't mean just clothes you think would look nice *on you*, I mean any that you think are pretty."

"If they wouldn't look nice on me then what's the point?" Holly demanded.

"The point is, dear friend, that I don't trust your judgement yet. Point out any pretty shops, OK?"

Holly reluctantly agreed and they continued on their way, wending between casual shoppers, groups of tourists and students on bicycles. Holly dutifully told Kat if she liked any of the shops that they passed and Kat appeared to be filing the information carefully. Once the last morsels of their ice creams had been consumed, Kat was ready. A woman with a plan, she grabbed her friend's hand and pulled her back to one of the shops that Holly had indicated. Stopping by the window, she pointed at one of the dresses,

"You like that one, don't you?"

Holly looked at her incredulously, "How did you know that?!"

"There's a theme to the shops you picked out. They all had delicate florals in the window in some shade of blue." In response to her friend's anxious look of enquiry, Kat continued, "It's a nice dress and blue suits you. Come on, let's go in and get a closer look."

The shop itself wasn't the standard high-street chain store, but instead was one of the many independent shops that Cambridge is blessed with. Holly had been into these shops before with her mother and had always enjoyed browsing the beautiful trinkets and handcrafted gifts on offer, but always with a certain detachment, as though she were looking at lovely things that might be a part of someone else's life. She felt totally uncomfortable standing there looking around at things for herself but it was also somewhat exhilarating. While Kat made a beeline for the back of the shop where all the clothing was kept, hanging on a long rail that bordered the whole back half of the room, Holly took her time getting there, admiring the mugs, pictures, vases and books that were all beautifully displayed where they might be glimpsed through the window. There were some beautiful earrings and necklaces featuring blue and white beads, almost like willow pattern china. Kat was right, Holly was drawn to blues. By the time Holly reached the back of the shop Kat had already reserved her a changing room and had a stack of dresses waiting, the blue floral from the window laid on top. Reaching to take it, Holly stopped.

"It's not the fabric I expected, it's too silky. I thought it would be a jersey or something."

"It's a beautiful fabric. Jersey is too warm for summer dresses Holly," Kat countered.

"But it's not stretchy, it'll feel uncomfortable."

"No it won't. I picked out the right size for you, it's

going to feel great." Kat wasn't going to bend on this. There was no way Holly was getting out of that shop without trying on every dress in the pile. Giving in to it with as little reluctance as she could manage Holly took the pile of clothes and stepped into the changing room.

Kat was right. It wasn't uncomfortable. The fabric didn't have any give to it but it didn't need it. It was a simple v-necked dress that nipped in to a fitted waistline and then flared out into a skirt that hung down gracefully from her hips. It wasn't loud or showy, just pretty and elegant and Holly felt beautiful in it. She pulled back the changing room curtain to get her friend's opinion, already knowing that the dress was coming home with her.

"Oh no! Dammit!" Kat looked distinctly put out. "Yes, whatever, it's perfect, you still have to try on the others! We are not done shopping yet!"

Holly laughed and pulled the curtain closed again. Now that she had her blue floral dress and the process had been so painless, an afternoon shopping didn't sound so bad.

So far from being bad, it actually turned out to be pretty wonderful. Holly of course purchased the dress, and some of the pretty willow pattern earrings, but she also found some other gems to add to her wardrobe. Two long floral skirts and some scoop neck t-shirts in white and grey to go with them, a pair of flat sandals in tan leather, a sage green cardigan in a lacy knit with cropped sleeves and, Holly's favourite purchase, a jumper. It wasn't the right weather for it of course but as soon as Holly saw it she couldn't resist. It was beautifully soft, a pale, creamy fawn colour and had a rainbow stripe right the way around the chest. It was this rainbow detail that had hooked Holly, it reminded her of the photos of her younger self and it felt right that some rainbow should come back into her life. Her final purchase was a print to go on the wall in her flat. It was a simple line picture, rendered in watercolour or possibly ink, and suggestive of a curved female form. Holly looked at the imperfect image of a woman, bending slightly as though just rising from a seated position, and she loved that it could look so blemished and incomplete and yet be utterly beautiful.

All in all, the day had been wonderful.

Chapter 22

On Friday Holly woke feeling rather flat. After the joys of the day before, a standard work day didn't hold its usual appeal. Surprisingly, Holly was actually looking forward to Sunday lunch at Rebecca's but the intervening days stretched out before her, void of entertainment. Holly decided that a second visit with Sandra might be in order. It might not lead anywhere but at least it would help her to pass the time with a greater feeling of productivity. After her talk with Joe it seemed increasingly likely that Terry had been killed by some shady member of the drug dealing community, if you could really call them a community, and that meant that Holly was very unlikely to track them down. Still, Holly didn't feel comfortable just walking away. There were so many niggling thoughts worming around in her brain now that she thought quitting the investigation cold turkey might be impossible.

Holly had already determined that she had no pretence or excuse for visiting Sandra again, so once she was done with her deliveries for the day she would go to the stables and just talk to Sandra outright. What was the worst that could happen?

Approaching the riding school a few hours later, Holly could think of lots of worst things that could happen. Most involved her being mortally injured by a huge, terrifying horse. Wishing that she'd brought Kat with her, snarky comments and all, Holly edged through the gates into the open area with stables on one side and the riding school's office buildings on the other. A teen in full riding gear approached from the stables and asked if she needed any help.

"Yes! Please! I'm looking for Sandra, is she working today?"

The girl chuckled good-naturedly, "She works every day! This place is her life! She's getting one of the riding classes going at the moment but she should be back soon. Do you want to wait in the office? I can tell her you're here once she appears."

"That would be brilliant, thank you!" Holly had turned towards the door indicated by the girl but turned back, "Have you been coming here long?"

"Yeah, three times a week since I was about six."

"Wow! That's a lot of dedication!"

"I love riding and this is the best riding school for miles. I went to one over in Chatterly for a bit when this place was closed but it's much better here."

"When was the riding school closed?"

"After Sandra's fall. She had to have surgery and she wasn't back up on her feet for a bit. She basically runs this place single handed so it had to close until she was better. I know she has a brother who helps out with the business side of things a bit, but all this," the girl gave an all encompassing gesture, "This is all Sandra."

Looking around her at the beautiful and efficient surroundings, Holly felt humbled. Sandra wasn't that much older than her, they had been at secondary school at the same time, just about. There was quite an age gap between Sandra and Joe. It was impressive that Sandra had managed to take on the riding school by herself and keep it going solo. Not quite solo though.

"Did you ever meet Terry Wood when he worked here?" she asked the girl.

"Terry Wood? No, I don't think so. I know everyone who works here and the name isn't familiar."

"He worked here for a while when the stables reopened, after Sandra's accident. He hasn't worked here in a while though," Holly remarked.

"Nope, sorry. I don't know him." The girl looked sincere and Holly supposed that their paths might just not have crossed. She had wondered if Terry had seen the riding club as another possible location with access to teenagers to sell drugs to, but really the horse riding set might not be the type.

"Ok, thank you. I appreciate the help," Holly told her.

The girl gave a smiling goodbye and continued on her way as Holly headed into the office to wait for Sandra. She entered cautiously, just in case a rogue equine lurked within, but she found the room blessedly empty of horses. There were however pictures of horses everywhere. Practically every inch of wall space was taken up with photos and drawings and paintings of horses. The only pictures that weren't horse related were photos of Sandra and Joe, together, beaming at the camera. Stood side by side the brother-sister resemblance was all the more noticeable. There was one picture of the two of them with an older couple who Holly thought must be their parents, but Joe was definitely in greater attendance. A series of postcards explained this anomaly. It seemed that the eldest two members of the Dawkins Family were on a world tour of sorts. There were postcards from America, from Belgium, from China, from India and a few that Holly couldn't recognise from the pictures. She was about to read one in greater depth when the sound of a throat being cleared behind her caused her to jump round guiltily. Sandra stood in the doorway, a look of impatient enquiry on her face. Not a good start.

"Hi! Sorry! I didn't mean to snoop, I was just admiring the postcards. So many incredible places!" Holly exclaimed.

Sandra stepped forward, her shoulders relaxed slightly but her manner still wasn't welcoming.

"My parents. They set off once they were both retired and they just kept going," Sandra told her.

"Sounds amazing. My parents travelled a bit before they settled down and had me and my brothers, but I can't imagine them doing anything like that now," Holly commented.

"They had Joe when they were young. Too young my mum always said. And me when they were too old. Neither of us was exactly planned, but we were both loved." Sandra smiled affectionately at the picture of the four of them all stood together.

"It looks like you and Joe are close, despite the age difference," Holly noted.

"Joe's amazing, he's always looked after me." Sandra took one of the photos of the two of them off the wall to look at it more closely.

"Why are you here?" Sandra suddenly demanded. The abrupt change in tone took Holly off guard.

"I wanted to ask more about Terry Wood. I felt like it didn't go well last time but I'm trying to find out everything I can..." Holly began.

"Why? Terry Wood wasn't a good person," Sandra snapped impatiently.

"Well maybe not but-"

"And you're not the police, it's nothing to do with you."

"Well no-" Holly admitted.

"And I told you everything I know. He didn't even work here long."

Holly took a deep breath and desperately tried to regroup and claw back a hold on the conversation.

"No, I know he didn't work here long but it seems like he never worked anywhere long. The girl I spoke to when I arrived said that she didn't even know him," Holly noted.

"Well he didn't work with the kids. I told you, he just did a bit of manual labour. He wouldn't be allowed to work with any of the riding students," Sandra explained.

"Really?" Holly asked with interest. Perhaps this was why Terry hadn't bothered to work here long.

"Really. To work with children you have to have all

sorts of checks done. Healthy and Safety certifications are everything in a business like this. If someone like Terry had worked here, worked with the children I mean, we could be shut down. Who would trust us with their children's safety then?" Sandra asked her.

It was a good point. Holly couldn't imagine allowing any child of hers near a horse at the best of times. With someone like Terry holding the reins? Never.

"No, that's a good point. When you say 'someone like Terry' what do you mean?" Holly asked her.

"What?" Sandra responded.

"Well, you said that Terry was a bad person. What makes you say that? Were you aware of his drug dealing?" Holly probed.

"Of course not! Not at the time I mean. I've heard about it now though, everyone has. It's been in all the papers since he was killed. The article said he was a drug dealer. I wouldn't have hired him to work here back then if I'd known. Like I said, it would risk the Riding School," Sandra told her.

"Right, but back then you still didn't let him work with the kids?" Holly asked again.

"No! I told you! You need to have all these checks and certifications to work with kids! Look, I'm really busy and I don't want to talk about this any more," Sandra told her finally, bringing the conversation to an abrupt close.

With that she strode from the room and Holly was left alone, again feeling like she'd just lost an argument she hadn't known she was having.

With one last look at the photos on the wall, Holly set off back to her van. She kept an eye out for stray horses but still kept up a swift pace. Despite the family resemblance Sandra didn't seem to have much of Joe's calm and easy going manner. It had not been a fun conversation and Holly was looking forward to getting back to her flat and winding down with a few episodes of whatever mystery show she could find on TV.

Chapter 23

Saturday mornings were always busy for Holly. The cafes needed enough stock to get them through the weekend and the deliveries took longer because of weekend traffic heading into Cambridge to explore the city's charms. As Holly wended her way through the busy streets, going slowly and carefully avoiding cyclists, she pondered the issue of Terry's bike. The alert was still programmed on her phone to inform her of any new bikes listed for sale in her town, but so far there had been nothing that could have been Terry's. A couple of children's bikes had been listed in the last couple of days but that was it. She still wasn't sure why it was relevant, it could be completely inconsequential, but she couldn't get it out of her head. Terry's bike should have been at his flat. If his rendezvous with the shady stranger was in the woods, he would surely have returned home at some point before that and left his bike on the rack in the hallway. Possibly he had gone straight to the woods and had left his bike there, but Holly hadn't seen any sign of it and neither had Kim. If it had been stolen then Holly would have expected to see it listed for sale by now. As she pulled up at her last delivery stop Holly had another thought. There was one more option that she hadn't considered and it would explain the bike's absence. Still, where was the bike now?

Saturday afternoons were a lazy time. After the frantic activity of the mornings she had a tendency to feel drained. Today was no different and even with the prospect of Sunday lunch at Rebecca's to look forward to the following day, Holly was still feeling lethargic and hazy. A nap would have been most welcome but Holly, as always, had baking to do. Rebecca had told her to bring a dessert with her to lunch and Holly wanted to prepare something wonderful. The weather was still glorious and it was to be an outdoor garden party so the decision practically made itself. Fishing out a book to remind her of the recipe, Holly ran through the list of ingredients for traditional strawberry shortcake with fresh whipped cream. She had everything that she needed so she got to work. Proper strawberry shortcake is somewhere between a cake and a biscuit. The flavour is deliciously buttery and the texture is dense and crisp. This provides the perfect contrast with the light as air cream and the beautiful, sweet strawberries. The cream and strawberries would need to be done just before setting off for the lunch, but the sponge could be made in advance. Shortcake is not your standard Victoria Sponge. It's made more like a scone and the result is a less fluffy cake. It feels counter intuitive the first time you make it but the first time you eat some you realise that it's actually a perfect concoction. Holly blended the butter, flour and sugar by hand until they formed a course breadcrumb consistency. This took some time as she had decided on a large, three tier cake, not knowing the numbers for the people attending the lunch. Once her breadcrumbs had formed, Holly added the egg and cream mixture and stirred it in until just combined. Too much mixing would create large air bubbles and that wouldn't be a shortcake. Once the mixture was just moistened through, Holly spread it into three cake tins and placed them in the hot oven for thirteen minutes. Thirteen minutes is, as it turns out, the perfect amount of time to decide that one cake isn't enough of a contribution to take to a garden lunch. Holly knew that Rebecca had a large family, what if there wasn't enough cake? What if there was a huge array of guests and some were left with no dessert whatsoever because Holly hadn't provided enough? Unthinkable!

By the time the oven timer sounded to let Holly know the shortcake was ready, she had already assembled the ingredients for chocolate chip cookies. A big batch of cookies should be enough to meet any deficiency in her proposed offering. While the shortcake cooled in its tins, Holly set about creaming butter and brown sugar. The trick to her perfect cookies was all in the beating time. People tended to mix the butter and sugar until just combined but Holly had discovered that extending the beating process up to seven minutes meant that the cookies were fully infused with the delicious brown sugar flavour that made them so addictive. Doubling up on the vanilla bean paste was another guaranteed win. Once the cookie dough was ready, Holly used her smallest ice cream scoop to carve out balls of chocolate studded dough and set them on a baking tray.

When the bowl was empty and the tray was covered in delicious domes, it went straight into the freezer. These would be baked tomorrow while Holly assembled the shortcake and she would have two wonderful dessert offerings all ready to go.

With her baking preparations complete, Holly found herself now at leisure to worry about the social side of the lunch. Rebecca was wonderful and Holly was sure that her family would be too, but she wasn't going to know anyone and socialising without the safety net of Kat's company wasn't something that Holly excelled at. She knew that if she dwelled on it too much she would work herself up into a total panic. To distract herself, she decided that dinner in front of the telly would be a good option.

Some meals called for comfort food. Holly grabbed some of her homemade pasta sauce from the freezer and set it in a pan to thaw. Next a pot of water went on to boil with a bag of penne waiting patiently beside it. Holly ate her meal curled up on the sofa with Diagnosis Murder on the television in front of her. She passed the evening in a haze of murder mysteries and went to bed early, still trying not to think about the plans made for her entertainment the following day.

Despite her early night Holly woke late, at least compared to her usual schedule. She only had a few hours before she needed to be at Rebecca's house so she headed straight to the shower to wash and condition her hair. As she made her naked dash to the airing cupboard to grab a towel on the way back to her bedroom, she was already running through her baking plans for the morning. She pulled on her standard garb of joggers and a t-shirt to do her baking in. She would change into her outfit for the day afterwards, as usual. She put the oven on to preheat while she made herself a cup of tea and a slice of toast. Once she'd munched her way through a couple of pieces of wholegrain, smothered with apricot jam and had slurped her last sip of tea, it was time to get to work.

The oven was now hot enough and she slid the first tray of cookies inside to bake. The shortcake was safely nestled in a tin, waiting to be piled with cream and fresh strawberries and she carefully transferred it to a plate ready. Placing all of the strawberries in her colander Holly rinsed them thoroughly under the tap before removing the stems, quartering them and then lightly sprinkling them with lemon juice and a little sugar. The juicy red berries were perfectly fresh and didn't need much sweetening at all, but it was a treat of a dessert and Holly wanted it to feel like such.

The oven timer indicated that the cookies were ready and Holly lifted them out and placed them on the side to cool and firm up before being removed from the tray. A second tray of cookies immediately replaced the first in the oven and Holly turned her attentions back to the cake. Pouring a long, steady stream of thick double cream into her electric mixer, she watched as it twisted and swirled in the bowl, becoming firmer and thicker. When it had reach the perfect point of forming firm glossy peaks, but not becoming so hard that it was ruined, she spooned one third of it onto the base of her cake, this was then topped with one third of the strawberries. She kept it as level as possible and then placed the middle round of her cake on top. Again the sponge was topped with a pillowy layer of cream and then the jewel bright strawberries. The final layer of sponge was added and similarly adorned and Holly turned the cake in a complete circle to check that it was perfect from every angle. It was absolutely beautiful and Holly placed it carefully in the fridge to keep it that way. The second tray of cookies was already out of the oven and Holly had to admit that it was time to get dressed.

It was with some trepidation that Holly collected the dress from her wardrobe, but it fitted just as perfectly as it had done in the shop. She teamed it with the willow pattern earrings, the lacy sage green cardigan and the leather sandals. It was a pretty outfit and Holly felt wonderful wearing it. It was the sort of thing she could imagine someone else wearing totally casually, but on her it was liberating.

The chocolate chip cookies went into one tin and the strawberry shortcake into another. She made two trips down to the van just to be able to carry the shortcake perfectly level. The drive was unspeakably tense. With every bump and turn Holly wondered if the cake would survive the journey intact. She thought that she had whipped the cream enough to hold everything together but she couldn't be sure. Pulling up outside Rebecca's house she immediately opened the tin and checked on the shortcake. Thank goodness! Still structurally sound. Stacking the cookie tin on top she lifted the two into her arms and made her way up the drive. It was only as she reached the door that she realised her conundrum. Her arms were both well and truly full and there was no way that she could knock on the door or ring the doorbell. Should she carefully lower both tins to the floor to free up her hands? Or she could risk the cake by trying to take the weight of both tins on one arm and possibly free up an elbow to knock with. Maybe she should just head back to the car and put the tins back on the front seat briefly. She was still pondering this, frozen with indecision, when she heard a muffled chuckling and to her relief, the door opened. Rebecca, like Holly, was in a floral dress though hers was a bright purple and she wore a white sun hat with a matching purple band. Her face was alive with happiness and Holly wouldn't have recognised her as the same woman who had answered the door last time she'd called.

Rebecca ushered Holly inside and straight to the kitchen, where she deposited her two tins carefully on the table. A man and woman of middle age were both stood at the kitchen counter constructing salads. Holly could hear at least a couple more people in the lounge arguing over what music to put on. There were about three more couples out on the patio and half a dozen children were playing on the lawn. Holly was glad that she had brought the cookies, one cake would not have been enough to feed all of these people. She needn't have worried however, once the tins had been opened and divested of their precious contents Rebecca led Holly, cake in hands, to the dining room. The chairs had been moved aside to make the dinner table into more of a buffet arrangement. It was piled high with food. There were pasta salads, potato salads, sandwiches, sausage rolls, quiches and some spaces marked out, reserved for hot food. The other end of the table was the desserts. Holly added her cake and Rebecca placed the cookies but there was also a trifle, a fruit salad, a loaf of lumpy looking banana bread and a small mountain of Rebecca's glorious lemon bars.

It was a spectacular feast and nervous as she might be, Holly was glad to have been invited. At least, for about five seconds she was.

"Right. Let me introduce you to my grandson," Rebecca announced.

"What?! Rebecca! I didn't agree to being set up!" Holly responded in alarm.

"Nonsense." Rebecca's tone brooked no discussion. "Of course you'll meet him. He's your age and you don't know anyone here, it only makes sense that I would introduce you. But you're right, I should introduce you to a few other people first so that it looks more natural."

"That's not what I meant!" Holly exclaimed.

"Don't worry dear, he's lovely. Now, come along!" And just like that Holly was swept out of the room. Rebecca introduced her to Mark and Denise in the kitchen and pointed out their children outside. Next were Dan and April who were out on the patio keeping an eye on their somewhat boisterous offspring as they played on the lawn. Charlotte and Evan were pointed out and waved to vaguely but everyone else was just ignored. Rebecca had clearly tired of pretence and was ready for the main event. Taking Holly by the arm she led her to the far side of the patio where three people were stood talking.

"Carol, Martin, you couldn't check on things in the kitchen could you? Just make sure everything is on track for food at one o'clock." And just like that Rebecca neatly disposed of the two smirking individuals that she considered to be surplus to requirements and she was left with Holly and a tall young man with sandy brown hair and an open friendly face.

"Holly, this is my grandson, Basil. Basil, this is Holly, she's a friend of mine." She stood smiling widely at the two of them while they awkwardly shook hands. Once she was satisfied that Holly wasn't going to run off, Rebecca began to back slowly away like a breeding specialist at the zoo. She had set the scene, made the introductions and now clearly she felt that all she needed to do was leave them to it and wait to be presented with more great-grand-children. Rebecca's intentions were so painfully clear that Holly was utterly mortified. If she could have willed the ground to swallow her whole she would have done so. The young man in front of her however seemed to be completely at ease.

Smiling openly at her, Basil launched perfectly happily into a friendly conversation.

"Lovely to meet you Holly, seems we at least have one thing in common. Were your parents keen gardeners too?" he asked her.

Being named Holly, this was not a comment with which she was unfamiliar, and yet there she stood, like a lemon, incapable of putting together an interesting sentence.

"No," she mumbled.

"Oh." His smile faltered a little in the face of such an unenthusiastic conversational partner.

"I mean, yes. They like gardening. But they actually named me after my grandmother on my dad's side," she explained in a rush.

"Ah! A family name! I wish I could say the same. Holly is a pretty name, not weird at all; you don't meet a lot of Basils though! And I really was named after a plant!" He was smiling his wide open smile again and Holly felt her own face respond in kind.

"So, my grandmother tells me that you're a baker?" he asked.

"Yes! I am! I provide cakes and things to a lot of cafes around here and some in Cambridge. I do the odd catering job too. Do you bake at all?" she asked, glad to have a topic of conversation in which she felt that she could hold her own.

He gave a slightly over the top grimace,

"Unfortunately that banana loaf in there is the height of my baking abilities. Honestly, I don't recommend you have some. I'm not a terrible cook, but I'm an absolutely rubbish baker," he cheerfully declared.

Holly laughed. His tone, though light, was sincere and Holly definitely believed him. When the time came however, she knew that she was going to have some of the banana bread.

"Have you always baked?" he asked.

"Pretty much, yeah. I started baking when I was little

and I sort of turned it into a business once I finished school."

"That's amazing! I can't imagine making a business for myself. I'm an office lemming unfortunately, never really done anything for myself."

"What do you do for fun then?" Holly asked tentatively.

"I draw a bit, read, watch too much TV..." he shrugged, "But that reminds me, you're the one Gran says is running round investigating murders aren't you?"

Holly blanched, she hadn't expected Rebecca to say anything about it and she wasn't sure how to explain what she was doing, getting involved in something like a murder case.

"Well, just the one. And I'm not really doing much, just asking questions and trying to figure out what happened," she told him.

"That sounds brilliant!" he enthused, "Tell me everything!"

"I really don't know much. I'm not working with the police or anything, I'm a bit like Miss Marple I suppose, it only works because I'm not a threat. People don't feel that they have to be careful what they say to a baker," she explained.

"Miss Marple?!" He looked at her sceptically. "More Miss Fisher, surely."

Beautiful, brave and glamorous, Miss Fisher was a much more complimentary comparison. Holly was so busy blushing that she almost didn't recognise the significance of Basil's words.

"Wait, you know Miss Marple? And Miss Fisher?" she

asked quickly.

"Of course! *Love* a mystery! So come on then, what have we got so far?!" His look of intense interest was too much to resist. Holly started at the beginning.

They had just reached Holly's second talk with Kim when lunch was announced. Everyone descended en masse on the table of food and Basil took Holly's arm to guide her through the fray. She enjoyed the feel of his hand on her elbow much more than she enjoyed the triumphant look Rebecca threw her as she piled her plate with chicken wings, salad and finger sandwiches. The room was a riot of clattering china, scraping cutlery, people calling dibbs on certain dishes, and parents ordering their children to eat more than just puddings.

Holly and Basil had been some of the first to reach the table and they navigated their way back out through the throng with difficulty. Once they had again gained the patio they made their way over to the low wall that separated the paved area from the lawn and perched next to each other by unspoken agreement. All the dishes had looked so incredible that Holly had gone for a little of everything. Rebecca's dinner plates were huge and Holly still felt that there had only just been space for her to sample all of the savouries and nab a piece of the banana bread, now balanced on the edge of her plate to keep it from getting a liberal dose of pesto. Holly suddenly wondered if she shouldn't have taken so much. It wasn't that there wasn't plenty to go round, but she vaguely felt that it would have been more ladylike not to load up her plate the way that she had. Looking over at Basil she decided not to worry. He was already working his way through the most enormous plate of food she had ever seen. He had piled his platter high with every type of food on offer including, she was pleased to see, a small slice of her cake and one of her chocolate cookies. He had already made a sizeable dent in his own meal and so Holly got to work on her own.

Once their initial hunger had been satisfied they continued eating at a more leisurely pace and resumed their conversation. Holly was vastly enjoying Basil's obvious admiration of her sleuthing and investigative abilities, though she wished that she had some more definite discoveries to tell him. By the time she had talked through everything that she had learned and run through all of her conversations with the people involved, Holly had long since finished her savoury food and Basil was nearing the end of his own. Holly was sure that he wouldn't be able to eat any more and that her beautiful desserts would go unappreciated but as soon as he finished his last drumstick he moved unhesitatingly onto his desserts with equal gusto.

"How can you eat so much?!" she exclaimed incredulously. She hadn't planned to ask it but she just couldn't see how it was possible. Basil was tall but thin. Most people would probably describe him as skinny, but Holly was watching him consume his own body weight in food without seeming at all phased by it.

She worried for a moment that she had insulted him but he just grinned, his kind face taking on a slightly goofy look of pride.

"Yeah, I eat a lot. It's terrible isn't it?! Apparently I've been this way since I was a toddler. Gran says I'd always eat anything I could reach."

"Well I'm impressed. If I ate that much I'd be the size of a whale. I just have this delicious looking piece of banana bread to go," she told him, indicating the lone item of food left on her plate.

Seeing it, he let out an unexpectedly booming laugh before burying his face in one hand.

"Don't do it! It's terrible! Everyone has to contribute but no one eats my banana bread! It's so awful!" he cried.

Holly determinedly took a bite and then her face froze. Gosh. That was... tangy. And what were those lumps made of? Flour maybe? And how did it manage that gritty texture at the same time?

"It's lovely," she told him.

Basil just smiled at her with an expression she couldn't quite identify. For a minute neither of them said anything and then he carried on in a cheerful manner that allowed Holly to catch her breath a bit.

"So, who's the murderer then?" he asked cheerfully.

"I don't know. It must be this shady character Terry was going to meet in the woods."

Basil laughed again,

"Shady character?! You do sound like a mystery show! That's a rubbish ending though. It leaves everything feeling unfinished. All these questions that haven't been answered."

"I know! Like, where's the bike!" she asked in

frustration.

"The bike? Is it important?" he asked her.

"I don't know. Possibly not. It could be though, depending on where it is. Or where it's been."

"I'm not following," he admitted.

Holly sighed. "Me neither really. I feel like there's so much I don't know. It's like everyone I spoke to pointed me one step further and then nothing really leads anywhere," she confessed glumly.

"Maybe that's intentional," he suggested. "Maybe someone has pointed you away because they have something to hide. What do you know for definite? Not what people have guessed at, but what you actually know for sure."

Holly took a deep breath and tried to sort through the facts.

"Terry couldn't hold down a job. He stole and he lied and he sold drugs. It doesn't seem like he had any kind of legitimate job at the moment. He was partly responsible for the death of Debbie Hall but we don't know if anyone knows that. He was friends with Joe. On the Tuesday he died it seems he was home in the morning with Kim before she left for work. He went to the youth centre to visit Joe. He was on his bike. He went from there to the woods, or possibly somewhere else first and then the woods. We don't know for sure, no one says they saw him between the two locations. He was next seen the following morning when my dad found his body," she finished.

"So there's a whole window of time that needs to be accounted for and this mystery man he met who needs to be identified. Do you know what direction he headed in from the youth centre?" Basil asked.

...

"Maybe you could talk to people and see if anyone saw him passing and see if he went anywhere before the woods," Basil suggested.

...

"Holly?"

"I don't think he did," she said finally.

"Sorry?"

"I don't think he went anywhere else before the woods. I think he went straight there and I think I've been an idiot," she told him.

Just then, as if by providence, the alert sounded on her phone.

"The bike! If I'm right and I can just find the bike, I think I can prove it. I set an alert for any bikes being listed for sale in town," she explained.

She pulled out her phone and checked the listing. There it was. It matched Kim's description perfectly.

Basil was now practically bouncing up and down beside her. "What is it?! Is it his?!"

"It is. That is unless someone happens to be selling one of the same make, model and colour, and that would be a bit too much of a coincidence I think."

"So what does that mean?" he asked eagerly.

"Nothing on its own. It depends who's selling it and where they got it."

Holly scanned the listing for contact details and found a

number listed at the bottom. She hesitated for only a moment before dialling.

"Hello? Yes, I'm calling about the bike for sale... yes, but actually I'm wondering where you found it... No, it's not mine... No, no I know that you didn't. Yes, my friend lost theirs and... yes? Yes of course... you're sure?... and what day was that?... Thank you. Yes, I'll talk to them and this will all get sorted out."

Holly hung up the phone and just sat staring down at it in her hand.

"What happened? What did he say?" Basil asked.

"God, this is awful," she said despondently.

"Was it not what you thought?"

"It was exactly what I thought."

"You really know who did it?"

"Yes, I really do."

"So what do we do now?" he asked her. It was the big question. She could do nothing. She could just leave it all alone and let the chips fall where they may. But what about her father? She couldn't let him continue as a suspect. And when it came right down to it, Terry Wood was dead. He was really dead. This wasn't one of her mystery shows, it was life and it might not be entirely fair but she couldn't just let it go.

She looked up into Basil's friendly face with its clear, green eyes.

"We call the police."

Chapter 24

"I don't know quite how to phrase this, because I really don't want to offend you, but are the police going to just believe you? I can't imagine they'll just jump to and arrest someone on the say so of a baker. Again, no offence intended whatsoever!"

Holly smirked at him. Gosh he was lovely: Rebecca was going to be insufferable.

"My brother is a policeman. I'll call him and he can handle it. Give me a couple of minutes, I'll be back soon," she assured him.

She made her way through the house and out to the front garden and rang Dan. She filled him in on everything that she had learned and what she had worked out from it. He was even less pleased than she had expected him to be about her impromptu investigations, but at least he took her seriously. When she told him who the killer was his reaction wasn't much different from her own. He told her not to do anything stupid and he hung up. Holly was at a loss. A big part of her still wished that she hadn't said anything about it. She sat down on the floor for a few minutes, trying to slow her heart rate. It had been a hell of a day all round. Heading back inside once she was a little calmer she found Basil waiting in the garden, pacing on the patio.

"Sorry to leave you waiting. I called Dan though and he's going to handle it," she told him.

"Dan is your brother?" he asked.

"Yes. Older than me though and he's been with the police for years now. He's a detective in London and he's going to contact the local officers to arrange an arrest. In fact he's probably done it already."

"So who was it? Who's the killer? It wasn't your dad was it?!" His look of comical dismay was enough to elicit a laugh from Holly, even given her current state of emotional turmoil.

"No it wasn't. But really, I didn't want it to be anyone. I probably sound stupid, but I didn't want anyone else's lives to be ruined over this."

"You don't sound stupid." He took her hand reassuringly, "You sound lovely."

Holly looked up at him and didn't know what to say. All she knew was that Kat was going to be over the moon.

The chirp of her phone pulled her back to herself and she pulled it out of her bag again to check the screen. She had a message from Dan, - "contacted local PD, arrest imminent."

She stared at it, frozen.

"Oh God."

Basil read the screen upside down and let out a tense breath.

"So that's that then."

"No. I can't let the police just show up without warning. What if there are people there? I'm going," she announced.

"What?" Basil looked alarmed now, "You can't!"

Holly stuffed her phone back in her bag and looked around her. Spying Rebecca she made her way over to her.

"This has been wonderful Rebecca, I'm sorry that I have to go but I do. It's an emergency." She dropped a swift kiss on the woman's crinkled cheek and fled.

She was out the house and almost to her van before she realised that Basil was with her.

"What are you doing?" she asked.

"Coming with you," he told her.

"You can't!" she insisted.

"If it's too dangerous for me to come with you then it's too dangerous for you to go," he countered.

They faced off for a minute, neither saying a word, then finally they both just clambered into Holly's van and set off.

When they pulled up at their destination the car park was full. Holly was glad that she had come, this didn't need an audience and maybe she could manoeuvre things so that it happened quietly.

Basil gave a sigh and she turned to look at him. He was staring at the building but turned to meet her gaze.

"I didn't know who it was until just now."

She'd forgotten that she hadn't even told him. He was coming with her none the less, no questions asked.

"You don't have to come in with me you know? I think I'll be safe," she assured him.

"If it's all the same, I think I'll tag along." He took her

235

hand for a moment before they exited the van and set off towards the building. Once inside they followed the sound of people. There was laughter and shouting from the hall to the right but a quick glance was enough to tell Holly that it wasn't what she was looking for. They continued along the corridor until they came to the door of an office, but it was empty. Where then?

Backtracking they came to the kitchen. Holly pushed the door open.

"Hello Joe."

He looked up from a fresh mug of tea, his usual wide, open smile spread across his face. Holly felt like she was about to cry. Tears threatened to fall but she held them back. His smile faltered.

They weren't alone in the kitchen, a few of the volunteers who helped out with sports classes were also there, similarly equipped with steaming mugs. They all turned and looked at her. She could feel their eyes and their questioning looks but she felt rooted to the spot. A hand slipped into hers and she felt Basil step forward beside her. His arm was warm against hers. She took a deep breath.

"Can I have a word Joe? I need to talk to you," she told him.

He hesitated, perhaps knowing that he would rather do anything else.

"We can go to my office," he suggested.

Basil spoke up now, "Outside would be better."

Joe nodded his understanding, "Yes, yes of course."

The three of them made their way out to the front of the building in awkward silence. Reaching the car park they all stopped, unsure of what to do now.

"I'm really sorry Joe." Holly's voice was small and Joe looked almost sympathetic at her obvious distress.

"I suppose the police are on their way?" he asked, his voice remarkably calm.

"Yes. They should be here soon," she confirmed.

"Well I appreciate the advance warning. Better like this than in the middle of a kids' sports session I suppose."

"Yes, that's pretty much what I was thinking," Holly admitted.

"I suppose your brother Dan gave you the heads up? I wonder what he'd do if I ran for it. He'd be in trouble I suppose," he said with a wry smile.

"Actually I gave him the heads up. I really am sorry Joe."

He looked at her puzzled for a moment before his face suddenly cleared and he gave a bark of laughter. "You solved it all?! Ha! That's brilliant!"

He was every bit the man who had given Holly her Girl's Third Place medal in tennis and beamed with pride even though there had only been three girls competing. It broke Holly's heart a little.

"It was all there. All the pieces. I think I just didn't want to see it," she said.

"I didn't want to do it... And I did want to." Joe sighed and ran his hands through his hair. "Well go on then, what is it they say? What gave me away?"

Holly shuffled her feet awkwardly, not sure how to explain.

"It just sort of suddenly clicked when I was talking about it today. The last of Terry's movements that we can really be sure of was him coming here. No one saw him after that. He didn't pass anyone on his way to some mysterious meeting, because he was already dead. If he'd gone home, his bike should have been there. The woods was so close he wouldn't have ridden his bike there from his flat. But of course, he hadn't gone home. You killed him here, in your office. When I came to see you and you gave me the catering job your office had been cleared, but not really. You'd cleared all of the surfaces and shoved everything into drawers so that any clean up would be simple. You could just wipe up any blood from the desk and floor. You got a rock from the woods beforehand and you had it ready in your office. You put it with the body so that everyone would assume he'd been killed there, in the woods. You thought that it would look like a drug deal gone bad. I accepted that without question but that's because we're naïve Joe. It turns out drug deals don't really happen in the woods at night. Kim said that there would be nothing more suspicious than two people meeting in the woods after dark. Drug deals are more low-key. It was like something from a movie. You just didn't know that because you've probably never bought drugs."

Joe was smiling somewhat ruefully which seemed to confirm Holly's words.

"But then that was something else. Something I should have questioned more. You don't do drugs and yet you were friends with a drug dealer. You were Terry's only friend actually. Except, you weren't, were you? You were never friends. When I talked to Sandra the first time, I mentioned your friendship with Terry and she scoffed. She was the only one who didn't know the lie because she would have seen right through it. If she had heard that you were friends with Terry she would have known right away that something was up."

Joe was looking darker now.

"I think that you did this for a lot of reasons Joe, but I think that mainly you did this for Sandra. I don't have any proof of this, and I'm not looking for any, but I think that Sandra bought drugs from Terry. I suspect it was because of the pain after her accident. Kim said that Terry worked at the stables for a bit but I think that was just a cover for him to supply Sandra with whatever drugs it was she was using. He hasn't been there in ages now, so I don't think that she's using them anymore, but that wouldn't matter would it? She would still lose the riding school. She told me that to work in a place like that you need all sorts of legal checks and certifications. I'm guessing illegal drug use wouldn't look good in the checks. You just wanted to protect your sister, didn't you?"

Joe said nothing but the storm raging inside was evident.

"And Terry used that against you? He blackmailed you. He made you recommend him for the job at the garage but then he stole. He made you refer him to some of the vulnerable elderly women that you know and then he stole from them too. And he made you let him hang around the youth centre even though he was selling drugs to the kids. It wasn't going to stop."

Joe slumped visibly. They could hear sirens in the distance now and as one they got up and started walking towards the sound to meet them up on the road. Joe didn't seem to bear Holly any malice. He had given it his best shot and it hadn't worked. Holly guessed that he'd made peace with the possibility of being caught before he even started. She hugged him goodbye before they put him in handcuffs and then she headed back to her van with Basil, not staying to watch Joe Dawkins bundled into a police car and carted off to jail.

It was only once she was back behind the wheel and had stopped hyperventilating that Basil spoke again.

"Will they be able to prove it do you think?" he asked her.

"Yes. They might be able to find some blood in the office or maybe in Joe's car, or there's the bike."

Basil looked at her questioningly.

"He'd forgotten about the bike. He didn't factor it into his plans. I noticed a broken bike lock on the ground when I was here on the Saturday and I didn't even think about it. I think Joe panicked when he recognised it as Terry's and realised that it linked Terry back here. He cut the lock and threw the bike in the industrial bin out the back. He probably thought he'd come back later and deal with it but the bin men picked it up before he could. It was the bin man who placed the ad online. He waited a bit, in case anyone put up fliers or online posts or anything, looking for a missing bike. When no one did he decided to sell it. When I spoke to him on the phone he confirmed that he found it here."

Basil let out a slow breath. He looked astonished and impressed but Holly just felt drained. The day was starting to fade and she felt like she could sleep for a week.

"He's not a bad person you know? Joe, I mean. When I told him that my dad was a suspect he invented the 'shady character' that Terry was going to meet. You were right. It did sound like something out of a mystery show."

"Because Joe made it up," Basil supplied, "Because he didn't want anyone else to get blamed for what he did."

"Exactly," Holly rubbed her eyes. "I should go to my parents. If they hear about this from Dan they might worry. Do you need a lift anywhere?"

"Back to Gran's would be good. I have my car there. I'm going to have to play it cool and pretend that her embarrassingly obvious set up isn't the best thing to have ever happened to me," he told her with a wide smile.

Even exhausted, Holly couldn't help but smile at that.

They drove in silence and Holly was grateful for it. Basil typed his number into her phone and gave her a quick kiss on the cheek before he left and Holly headed straight to her parents' house.

Dark had really fallen by the time she arrived and the golden glow of the windows had never looked so inviting. Before she could even reach the door however, it burst open and a torrent of noise hit her.

"I VERY CLEARLY SAID NOT TO DO ANYTHING STUPID! YOU CONFRONTED A MURDERER!!!"

Dan barrelled across the drive and pulled her into his arms. She was six years old again and crying into her brother's jumper.

As the sniffling slowed he set her down and looked her in the face as though waiting for her to explain why she had broken his favourite toy plane.

"Joe's going to prison."

Dan sighed, his stern expression softening slightly. He put an arm around her shoulders and guided her into the house. Within seconds her mother and Kat both had their arms around her and were checking her for injuries. They settled her at the table and two minutes later her father had swept away the wine glasses and placed tea and biscuits in front of her. She of course had to go through every detail again but it was easier this time. When she had finished they all just stared at her stunned. Dan looked absolutely furious but it turned out not to be at her.

"The local police weren't even looking for his bike! Apparently no one realised it might be significant!"

Kat smiled at her best friend, full of pride. "Someone realised."

Half a mug of tea had gone some way towards reviving Holly and she suddenly noticed the unusual situation she had walked into.

"Dan? What are you doing here?" she asked suddenly.

"I was already in town when you called," he told her.

"What? Why?"

She looked from beaming face to beaming face. When her eyes finally reached her friend, Kat held up her hand to display the beautiful solitaire ring on the third finger. Without another thought Holly flung her arms around her best friend. Whatever this meant for her, for Kat and Dan it was wonderful news.

Sitting back in her chair Holly smiled at her brother, but it was Kat who took the lead of course.

"Dan decided it's time to settle down. He realised that since he had the good fortune to win himself the most beautiful, wonderful, intelligent and capable woman ever created, it only makes sense to make it official," she explained with a grin.

Dan gave a half shrug half nod, "Yes, that's pretty much it. Besides, there's a senior position available in the local station and it's obvious they need the help."

Holly looked from Dan to Kat, to Dan, to Kat, and back to Dan.

"Wait. You're staying?! Here?!"

"Of course!" Kat assured her friend, her smile even wider than ever. "Why would we leave?! Now, we just need to find you a date for the wedding."

"Actually," Holly smiled slowly, "I think I have one."

Acknowledgements

Creating this book has been the realisation of a dream that I've been quietly nurturing for a couple of decades.
I am so grateful to have had the opportunity to actually sit down and write it after all this time.

A big thank you goes to my wonderful mother for being one of my first readers and such a fantastic editor. I appreciate every suggestion and every correction to my less than perfect grammar.

Thank you to my brother. He supported me through the writing of this book, trading our work back and forth and urging each other on with much needed praise.

Last but not least, thank you to my incredible husband for giving me the time and freedom to write and for making sure that I never felt, even for one moment, like I might not be able to do this.

Printed in Great Britain
by Amazon